Understanding & Encouraging
YOUR CHILD'S ART

Also by Mia Johnson:

Everything You Want to Know About Drawing and Painting

The Pink Heart and Other Tamperings

Teach Your Child to Draw

Understanding & Encouraging

YOUR CHILD'S ART

How to Enhance Confidence in Drawing
Ages 2 to 12

Mia Johnson

Lowell House
Los Angeles

Contemporary Books
Chicago

Library of Congress Cataloging-in-Publication Data

Johnson, Mia, 1949-
 Understanding and encouraging your child's art : how to enhance
 confidence in drawing : ages 2-12 / Mia Johnson.
  p. cm.
  ISBN 0-929923-73-1 (case edition)
  ISBN 1-56565-099-9 (paperback edition)
 I. Title.
 BF723.D7JJ64   1992
 155.4-dc20   92-5919
                                                         CIP

Lowell House
2029 Century Park East, Suite 3290
Los Angeles, CA 90067

Publisher: Jack Artenstein
Vice-President/Editor-in-Chief: Janice Gallagher
Director of Publishing Services: Mary D. Aarons
Design: Preview Graphics, Inc.

Manufactured in the United States of America
10 9 8 7 6 5 4 3 2 1

Drawings are potent indicators of how children grow and develop. With little preparation and no hesitation at all, children hurl themselves at sheets of paper and embark on personal odysseys of discovery, charting their way with crayons or felt pens or whatever is handy.

Mia Johnson is a sympathetic observer and sometimes a participant in these odysseys. She also has a mission of her own: to reacquaint parents with behaviors that were once second nature to them, when they were as old as their children, but that have long since been allowed to lapse. She makes it her business to instruct and advise her readers and, in the process, help them to reenter the world of the child.

That she succeeds so well in this book may be attributed to her writing style, which is direct and uncluttered; and to the approach she takes, which is sensible without being sentimental. The result is a book which deals directly with the experiences of children, and with the experiences of parents as they attempt to interpret the artifacts of their children's exploration. As you read *Understanding and Encouraging Your Child's Art*, you will find your head nodding in agreement with what Mia Johnson has to say. And in the end, when you put this book down, you will be not only better informed but also impressed, all over again, by the power and charm of children's graphic expression.

Dr. Ronald MacGregor, Department Head,
Visual and Performing Arts in Education
University of British Columbia

Contents

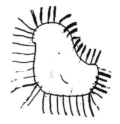

"Look What I Made for You, Mom!"

A design of houses by Eddie, age 6 years, 2 months

Young Johnny runs into the house, shouting, "Look what I made for you, Mom!"

He thrusts a crumpled paper at his mother, who gazes, somewhat bewildered, at the maze of lines and shapes on it. "Oh," she says, "that's nice, dear. What is it?"

"I dunno!" Johnny calls back as he runs out the door. His mother is left holding the picture, wondering what it means and whether or not she should keep it.

Has this scene happened in your home? Every day our children collectively make tens of thousands of drawings and pieces of artwork. It is hard for parents to know what to make out of most of them – not to mention what to do with them!

Understanding and Encouraging Your Child's Art is designed to help you understand and support your child's efforts. With the exception of certain problematic stages (which will be discussed in detail later in the book), I believe that children know exactly what they are doing when they make a picture. Sometimes it is we, the adults, who may be out of touch with their ideas. We need to understand that children go through certain identifiable stages in their own conception of what a picture is, and how it should be organized. Children appear to create their own challenges as they draw, and the schemes they work out to solve their problems may have nothing in common with the way things look or behave in the "real world." If we can understand and reinforce their ideas at the appropriate times, I believe most children will experience continued success with drawing and all forms of art that are dependent on problem solving – right into adulthood.

When I began the process of collecting material for this book, I sat down with children ages 2 to 12 as they drew the pictures. It was very important to observe first-hand the mental and creative processes of the children and listen to them as they described what they were trying to do. As you will see when you look through this book, it is often difficult to really appreciate children's drawings after the fact. (It's a little bit like what I later describe as trying to understand a rodeo by looking at the hoofprints left behind in the dust.)

After hundreds of hours observing children draw and hundreds of drawings, I began choosing examples that would best convey some of the more obvious problems, solutions, interests, and beliefs that I found most of the children had. None of the examples, however, is what might be considered an award-winning drawing. I wanted to show you only perfectly ordinary, everyday drawings to help you under-

Figure 1. A drawing by Margaret, age 2 years, 10 months.
The lines and shapes your child draws when he scribbles . . .

stand the perfectly ordinary drawings your *own* child may be doing every day.

In this book, I have organized the chosen drawings into ten sections representing the general stages or phases I believe most children go through: scribbles, shapes, designs, early pictures, scenes, separate objects, realism, cartoons, and action. Each of the children's drawings is accompanied by a brief description of the formal elements, such as how the drawing was made, how the parts were organized, and what the different parts meant to the child who drew it. By understanding drawings that look similar to those drawn by your own child, you will begin to recognize and follow your child's development with interest. Many of the descriptions for understanding each drawing have "artistic" developmental clues that will point to your own child's progress.

In most cases, a brief conversation I had with the child about his or her drawing follows the description, and includes tips on how to talk to your own child at a similar stage. What children, especially young ones, say and do as they draw is often more important than *what* they draw. As a parent or teacher, you are in an enviable position to make comments about your child's or student's drawings either as they are created or shortly thereafter. Your comments can support and validate the child's ideas, and in this book I have suggested ways you can do so.

Finally, I have provided various practical suggestions for encouraging your child in his artistic development. These include ideas for drawing games, tips on saving or displaying drawings, suggestions for motivating waning interests or helping your child through problem phases, and advice on appropriate art materials at different ages.

Understanding and Encouraging Your Child's Art is designed so you can skim through it and look for drawings that match your child's. You can also read about drawings by children who are younger or older in order to see where your child is coming from and where he or she might be going. At the end of each of the nine sections, you will find questions that parents and teachers frequently ask me. I hope my answers will shed some light on concerns you may have about your own child.

It seems as if we are always waiting for our children's drawing to be "about" something else. When our children are toddlers, we wonder when they will stop scribbling. When they begin to draw shapes, we wonder what the shapes mean. And when they begin to draw pictures, we wonder when they will start to look "real."

In their middle years, we wonder if our children are talented. If our older children draw cartoons, we wonder why they don't do *real* drawings. And so on.

I have written this book because I believe each stage of your child's drawing development is very precious, and it will never come again. I hope this book will help you enjoy your child's drawings during every one of them. Perhaps, after all, Johnny only intended his maze of lines and shapes to be a maze of lines and shapes.

Figure 2. … are still lines and shapes when his drawings become recognizable.
A drawing by Daniel, age 4 years, 9 months

Scribbles

Beginning to Control Lines

Separate lines and zigzags show the beginning of control by Kevin, age 2 years, 10 months

Scribbling is where all drawing begins. Scribbles can be composed of many different things, including circular loops, runaway lines, and up-and-down and back-and-forth zigzags, repetitions, or overlapping. They can also indicate places of emphasis in the drawing. Whether your child makes these marks with energy or rhythm or moves her crayon at random on the paper, her scribbling is always an active exploration of marks on a surface.

From about 10 to 18 months of age, the infant child is busy making a connection between the crayon in her hand and the marks it makes – or doesn't make – on the paper, the wall, the furniture, or the family dog. It appears to her that the crayon is making the marks rather than she herself, and she is simply following along.

Your child begins to *draw* when she becomes aware that she is the one in control of the marks that she makes. In the transition stage from infant to "drawing" child, she will become interested in the pressure of her crayon, hard or soft, and whether it will go right through the paper if she presses hard enough. She will cover large areas of surface with crayon just to cover large areas of surface. At whim, she will experiment with many different colors, colors that by adult standards do not necessarily "go" together and may not match the colors of objects in the real world. She will begin to vary the pace of her drawings, producing some marks quickly and others slowly.

Most important, she will start to think about the edges of the paper as a "container" for her marks. This is not to say that she can or will contain her marks; she is just beginning to see the edges of the paper as a possible place to stop.

Between the ages of two and four, your child will start drawing in a very intuitive way, "feeling" that something needs to be marked over here and something else scribbled over there. For example, in figure 3, Ruth intended to fill in one corner of the paper but not the opposite corner. In figure 4, she meant to scribble right in the center of the page and to leave the rest of the paper blank. She didn't see these drawings as unfinished.

The appearance of your child's scribbles will gradually become more controlled during her third year, and this stage is where this book begins. If you follow closely, you can see how the scribbles start to take the form of different line types. First come the zigzags, then the separate lines, long or short, followed by areas of repeated dots. Interest in emphasizing areas of her drawing will increase, and the emphasis will

Figure 3. A drawing in the corner by Ruth, age 2 years, 6 months. The corner of the paper is a "container" for these marks.

Figure 4. A drawing in the middle of the paper, also by Ruth. The space around it contains and suspends the drawing.

become more obvious to adults. A three-year-old will begin to cross her separate lines and may develop a very tidy zigzag line. The edges of the paper clearly act as a container for her compositions, and she may elaborate them with a border. I don't think there is a more fascinating stage of children's artistic development than this one. I encourage you to collect your own child's scribbles over a period of time, and I hope you will agree!

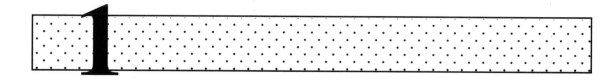

Understanding Sarah's drawings

During these early years of your child's development from random to purposeful scribbling, you may not see any obvious consistency or even progress in your child's drawings. "They all look the same to me," you might think, or "He doesn't draw yet, he just scribbles." But take a close look at the next three pictures with me.

Taken alone, each one may almost look like the next one: just scribbled lines. There are certainly no people or buildings or anything else realistic here. But they are actually quite different, and together they show the natural development of one child over a period of 14 months.

Figure 5 is a typical drawing from Sarah's third year of life. Although it doesn't resemble anything, and although it's not particularly attractive, it was nonetheless very pleasurable for her to do. Several different colors were used on top of one another. The loops go up and down or at an angle across the page. What a challenge to draw with such freedom and yet retain enough control to stay on the paper!

Figure 6 was drawn shortly after and is typical of about 150 other drawings done in the same time period. Sarah was nearly three years old and extremely productive and energetic. Notice how much more control she shows. The lines can be divided into three groups: two are up-and-down or vertical groups, with one horizontal group crossing them. I have called these lines groups, although each of the three groups is actually made with one or two continuous zigzag lines.

Within a year, Sarah developed enough control to draw each line separately. Figure 7 is a lovely arrangement of a number of separate vertical lines which she had carefully placed along one strong horizontal line. Her ability to do this is a result of her natural mental development as well as her earlier experiences with placing lines, repeating gestures, and organizing space. In the beginning, there is nothing else.

Talking about scribbles

At this age or stage, your child is drawing frequently and rapidly. You may be surprised to see her do five or more drawings in less than two minutes. If you feel inhib-

Figure 5. Random scribbling by Sarah, age 2 years, 6 months

Figure 6. Zigzag lines in two directions by Sarah, age 2 years, 9 months

ited yourself about drawing, her output may seem even more amazing. There is a great tendency to say, "Slow down! Draw something nice – don't just scribble!" However, your child is not aware that there is any other way to draw. She does not know what you know; she only knows what she knows, and what she knows unfolds as she does it. Your child is truly self-taught at this stage. Every day she builds on the last.

There is also a great deal of regression, or seeming to go backwards. Just when you think she has finally stopped "scribbling" and is starting to make "real lines," your child may scribble nonstop for several weeks or months. Be kind, be patient, and say little. I try to limit the little I do say at this stage to "Why, thank you," "What a pile of colors you made!" or "You've made a lot of lines."

Suggestions for parents of scribblers

■ Give your child lots of opportunities to experiment on different sizes and types of surfaces. Match the size of the drawing medium to the size of the surface: small crayon to small paper, and large crayon to large paper. Buy large sheets or rolls of paper and superwide felt pens; bathtub crayons and paints; and large outdoor sidewalk chalks. Buy 8½" x 11" bond paper by bulk in a 500-sheet package, and offer your child washable markers and pencil crayons.

■ Collect your child's drawings over a period of time, and mark each one on the back with her age in years and months rather than with the date. Every six months, mount two or three drawings in your family photo album. You can arrange the rest of the drawings on the floor and take a photo of them for your album.

■ Look at the drawings by other children in your child's day care, play group, or preschool, and take an interest in their development, too. You will be surprised at all the variations on what at first looked like "just scribbles."

■ Let your child choose his own drawings for display. If you put them on your refrigerator, let him attach and change the drawings himself, using magnets, even if you end up with several layers of drawings.

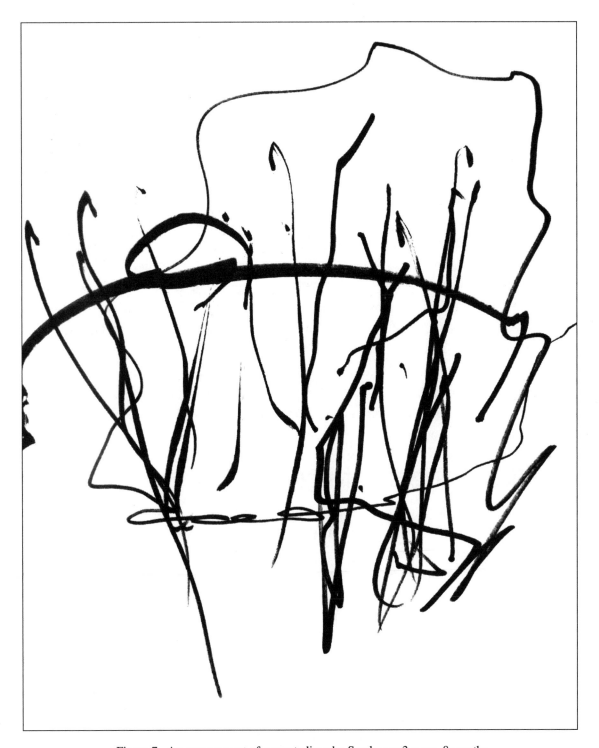

Figure 7. An arrangement of separate lines by Sarah, age 3 years, 8 months

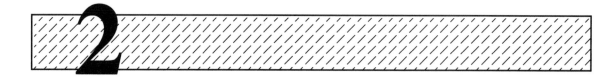

Understanding Jordan's drawings

Not all scribbles are created equal. There are enormous differences between the scribbles of different children and sometimes even between scribbles created by the same child on the same day. The drawings in figures 8 and 9 are good examples of different scribbles by the same child.

Figure 8 has loose and wandering lines that travel in a continuous loop drawn diagonally from the bottom left corner of Jordan's paper up toward the top right corner. Place your finger on any loop and follow the line as it winds lazily toward the center of the paper. A bold, curved line surrounds the loops on the right side and stops them from traveling any farther.

If you follow any line in figure 9, you will experience quite a different feeling. Unlike figure 8, each line in figure 9 is separate. The straight lines are crossed in a grid on the right, forming squares. An emphatic zigzag enters from the left. Only the dark, emphasized patch of lines is similar in both pictures.

Talking with Jordan about his drawings

When you talk to your child about his drawings, be very specific. Say "line," "zigzag," or "dot." Describe what the lines *do*, rather than anything they might stand for. You might say they "travel," "wander," "loop," "stop," "repeat themselves," or "make rows." Try to tell your child how his drawings make you feel as well. I might follow a line in figure 8 with my finger, for example, and tell Jordan, "Look at this line go loop, loop, loop, right into the middle. That makes me feel dizzy!"

Suggestion

■ Be careful not to throw out your child's drawings where he might see them. Each drawing is very meaningful to your child. It is a whole new thing he created all by himself which never existed before. He is not critical enough to tell the "good" from the "bad," or from what adults might think is an incomplete drawing.

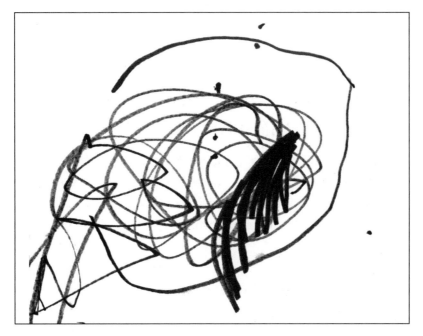

Figure 8. A looping composition with an emphasized
area by Jordan, age 4 years, 5 months

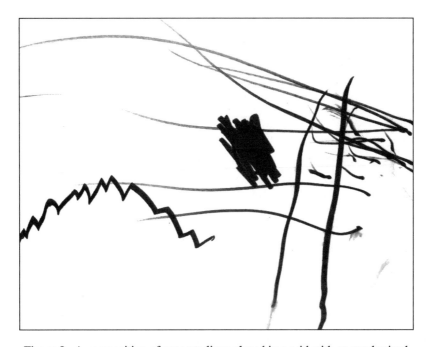

Figure 9. A composition of separate lines placed in a grid with an emphasized
area, done by Jordan on the same day as the drawing in figure 8

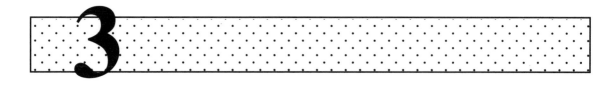

Understanding Elska's drawing

At some point your child may become quite enchanted with making dots. Imagine the sense of control and precision she must feel! By poking briefly and specifically at the paper, she can make a brief and specific record: a dot. It is hard to stop with just one dot. Scribbles, designs, and early pictures are often punctuated with groups of dots.

Figure 10 shows very controlled scribbles on several different areas of the paper. On the left, a vertical line is carefully crossed with a row of shorter, horizontal lines. The vertical lines on the bottom right have a definite cross. There is pattern of dots that move clockwise up to the brief zigzag scribble in the top left corner. If you cover any of these areas with your hand, you can see how the drawing becomes unbalanced.

Suggestions for scribble games

Once your child is able to make different kinds of lines and can control when she stops and starts her lines, she will be delighted to play some simple drawing games with you. Here are two ideas:

■ "Simon Says." Use two pieces of paper, one for you and one for your child. You be "Simon" or the leader first. Whatever you do, she will do. If you say, "Simon says, Go dot-dot-dot," draw three dots and wait for her to do the same. Or say, "Simon says, Go really long [or short or little, big or tall, or loop]." Let your imagination go and make different kinds of lines. Then let your child be "Simon."

■ "Follow the Leader." For this game, you and your child will share a piece of paper. You will each need a different color pen. Begin by being the leader and drawing a continuous line slowly. Your child will put her pen on the paper behind yours and follow you. If you make a loop, do it gradually so she can follow. Make a zigzag of "stairs" for her to climb. Make dots or broken lines. Then let her be the leader.

Figure 10. An arrangement of lines and dots by Elska, age 3 years, 7 months

Questions & Answers

My four-year-old son wastes a lot of paper when he draws. He only puts a few lines on each piece and says he's finished. I can't get him to draw longer.

Your son's attention span may only be a few seconds or a minute long right now, which is quite normal. If he says he's finished, he probably is! Buy him paper in large amounts at a discount stationery store or copy center.

■

Whenever I try to put up one of my two-year-old's drawings he screams and runs away with it. Why won't he let me display them?

The idea of displaying art doesn't make much sense to very young children, who are really only interested in making it. Ask him what he'd like to do with the finished drawings.

■

My three-year-old brings a lot of collages and art "projects" home from day care, but she and the other children don't seem to actually draw very much. Should I say something?

If your child attends a day care that encourages parent participation, you could offer to give a drawing class once a week for 15 or 20 minutes. If the people in charge agree to let you try, buy 8 1/2" x 11" paper in 500-sheet packages and a box of pencils or washable felt pens. Tell the children they can draw whatever they like. Listen to them as they work. At the end of each class you could tack up some drawings (including scribbles) to talk about. Use the "Talking about this drawing" sections of this book as a guide.

■

My two-year-old daughter covers her arms and face with paint or felt pens. Will they hurt her skin?

To be on the safe side, always be sure to buy paint and pens that are marked "wash-

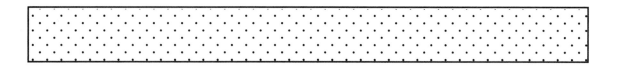

able" and "nontoxic." But if she would rather paint her face than a piece of paper, why not buy face paints for her instead?

■

My son is three, and when he draws he bangs his pen so hard that he only makes dots. How can I get him to slow down?

Dotting is a natural stage, and he may be enjoying the sensation. For a slower activity, try a "rubbing." Put large coins, paper clips, or upside-down leaves under a piece of drawing paper. Show him how to rub a pencil or wax crayon on the paper to make an impression of the objects underneath.

■

Our three-year-old daughter is already drawing figures and scenes. Is she very advanced?

Yes. Children's drawing are a good indication of their cognitive organization and their mental-motor coordination. However, please don't be disappointed if her development levels out; this is very common as children learn new things!

■

My child does so many drawings each week, I don't know which drawings I should keep and which I should throw away. I can't keep them all! What do you recommend?

Talk to your child while he is drawing or soon after. Write a brief comment on the back about what he was doing and make a note of his age. Keep as many drawings as you can for a few months, then weed out the "keepers" and start again. Time will give you a better perspective on what to keep as you begin to see patterns of development in his drawings.

Shapes

Learning to Enclose Lines

Large shapes containing small shapes by James, age 5 years, 11 months

As your child grows and develops, he will soon teach himself to draw not only separate lines but separate shapes as well. All by himself, he will develop a kind of shorthand. Instead of creating a shape by filling in an area with a scribble, he will discover that he can simply draw the outline of the shapes. At first, his outlines will consist of different kinds of circles, which may be long and thin, roundish, or experimental like those in figure 11. Your child is actually learning to *bend* a line as he draws it until it *closes* itself. This is a major accomplishment and the next big step to watch for after he learns to make separate lines.

You may first notice these odd-shaped simple outlines as they begin to appear among less controlled scribbles in your child's drawing (see figure 15). He will also continue to scribble, apparently without purpose, for some time after these shapes first appear, so don't be surprised. He is just taking his time sorting things out.

Eventually he will teach himself to vary, repeat, combine, or overlap these simple outline shapes. His interest in separate lines will grow, and he will teach himself to stop and start lines and curves. He will become aware not only of the outside edges of his paper but also whether the paper is in a vertical (up and down) or a horizontal (across) position. In his fourth year, your child will begin to combine the newfound outline shapes with more purposeful scribbling (perhaps for "filling in" shapes and areas) and with larger container shapes and borders.

At about age five, your child will enter what I call a "visual casserole" stage in which all the ingredients for real pictures begin to appear and are seemingly combined on purpose. At this stage most parents are quite tempted to believe that their children's drawings really stand for something. Your child may even be encouraging you by giving names to his drawing, especially if he has frequently been asked "What is it?" However, you will have to be satisfied for now that the way the shapes are combined or arranged is meaningful all by itself!

Figure 11. Experimental shapes based on "circles" by three- and four-year-olds.
Clockwise from the top left: an enclosed zigzag; a long thin circle that is colored in;
two circles overlapping; and circular shapes inside circular shapes

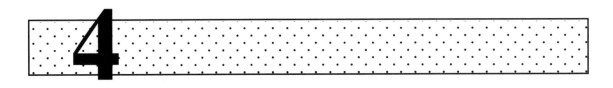

Understanding Steve's drawings

Figure 12 represents three-year-old Steve's earliest efforts to draw circles. If you put your finger on any line (with the exception of the short crossover lines) and follow it, you will wind your way back to where you started. This is Steve's first understanding of a circle: it is a loop, or a curve, that keeps going until it encloses itself. He had an *intent* to come back and close it as he drew.

Steve's drawing in figure 12 shows a number of overlapping circles. At the time, he may not have been aware that he was overlapping them. He may have been just making them, one *after* another, and they happened to be one on *top* of another when he was finished.

Figure 13 also shows repeated circles, but in this drawing they appear to have been arranged quite purposefully. Notice how there is a similar width of space between the circles on the left-hand side. Steve was likely drawing with the intention of keeping the circles apart, which takes great control.

Beginning at the bottom of the middle circle in figure 13 and continuing counterclockwise up to the top right (which is partially covered with vertical scribbles) are about seven short crossover lines. This is a crucial step in Steve's drawing development. By crossing over a line, he is learning about changing direction. He can now teach himself to *interrupt* the flow of a line or curve and to "build" on his own lines; he can now learn new patterns for line placements. These patterns will soon lead him to put "rays" on a circle to make a sun and to draw "legs" on a circle to stand for a man. But most of all, by stopping to cross one line over another, Steve is teaching himself that he is the one in control of his drawing and whatever lines appear. *He makes them himself, all by himself. They do not exist before he makes them.*

No wonder children love to draw! Just think of all the possibilities for making, controlling, and combining an endless number of lines. Figure 14 shows a different arrangement of circular shapes, three of which are carefully filled with dots. This takes practice and control.

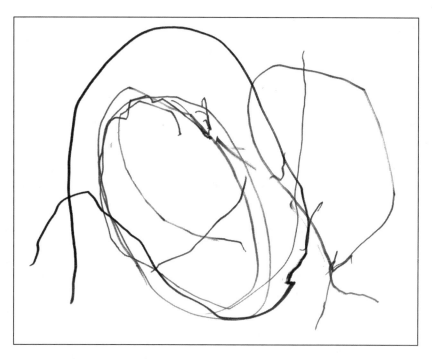

Figure 12. A "pile" of circles by Steve, age 3 years 2 months

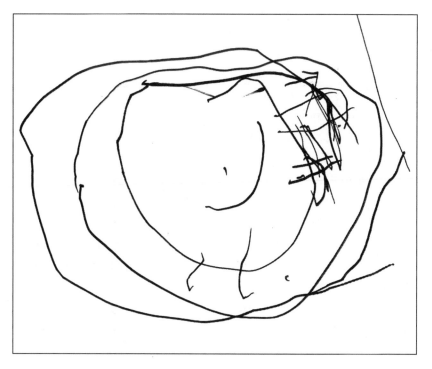

Figure 13. An arrangement of circles by Steve on the same day as figure 12

Talking with Steve about his drawings

Steve told me that figure 13 is a "face." Certainly there are two dots and two areas of scribbles, either of which could be "eyes"; there is a short curved line in the middle of the drawing which might be a "mouth"; and the two crossovers at the bottom might be early "legs."

Wishful thinking or not, Steve has included elements typically found in early faces, although he has not placed them as obviously as he might in his later drawings. It is as though he has said to himself, "These are the things that I know faces have, so I'll just pile them in here," like a visual casserole of face parts.

I responded by agreeing, "Yes, you did put in all of the things that belong to a face."

Suggestions for parents of children drawing shapes

■ If your child is also at an early stage of exploring shapes and combining them, be as encouraging as possible. Keep piles of paper and a jar of washable felt pens out and ready wherever he tends to spend a lot of time sitting. This may be on the kitchen table or counter, on a table near the television, or both. You are trying to put as few obstacles as possible between his impulse to draw and the materials he needs to do so. Well-meaning parents of preschoolers often buy an easel and art supplies but install them three rooms away where the child would have to be alone to use them. If your child wants *your* company, and if you happen to spend a lot of time in the kitchen, then that's an ideal place for him to work, too.

■ Although it may be hard at first, try to keep your comments about his drawing very neutral and abstract. Your child will understand what you mean if you say, "This shape is really *large* for the paper," "This shape is much *smaller* than that one," "That's a really *long* shape you made at the bottom," or "Hey, you put three things together!"

■ Change the drawing medium weekly. Put out a jar of washable felt pens one week, a jar of crayons the next, a jar of colored pencils the next. Then start over.

■ Put out a supply of paper 8½" x 11" or smaller.

■ Keep a notebook handy; the paper can be lined or unlined. Do not make him fill the pages in order. When every page has a drawing or a scribble, write the month and the year on the front cover of the notebook.

Figure 14. Three circles filled with dots by Jason, age 3 years, 8 months.
Notice how each corner of the paper is marked with a dot as well.

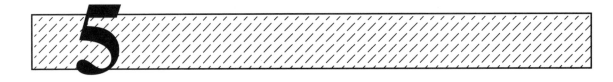

Understanding Laurel's drawing

Figure 15, by four-year-old Laurel, is a good example of many kinds of early shapes and lines as well as their composition or placement on the paper. Laurel had been doing variations of drawings like this one for five months and during that time she worked out many of her ideas about shapes and their placement.

You can squint your eyes at this drawing in order to see the main lines. There are several large circles (or ovals) slightly overlapping one another, drawn almost to the width of the paper. Some of these circles are incomplete, but together they form the outline of a large enclosed space. Within this oval space and seldom breaking out of it are numerous scribbles, dots, and line crossovers. You can see a small grouping of line crossovers on the far right side of the oval. The drawing is completed by five precise smaller shapes along the top of the drawing, slightly overlapping the large oval mass.

It is also interesting to note two straight lines near the middle bottom of the drawing, which Laurel had been adding to many of her oval shapes in recent weeks to denote "legs" or "feet."

Laurel used several different colored pens and pencils in the original drawing, which has been reproduced here in black and white. Her most *definite* lines – the five small shapes along the top and the large oval with crossovers on the right – were done with her favorite color, purple. Heavier, firmer, and more decisive, these lines appear much less "experimental" than many of the squiggles and scribbles to the inside left of the mass.

Watch for small "floating" shapes, similar to the ones in figure 15, among the controlled scribbles in your child's drawings. This is an important and exciting stage of development, with designs and pictures soon to follow. In figure 16, Christopher drew an enclosed line around a printed border as a kind of frame for his design of scribble patches. His line is like a large circle that wraps the printed border. He is becoming aware of the use of shape.

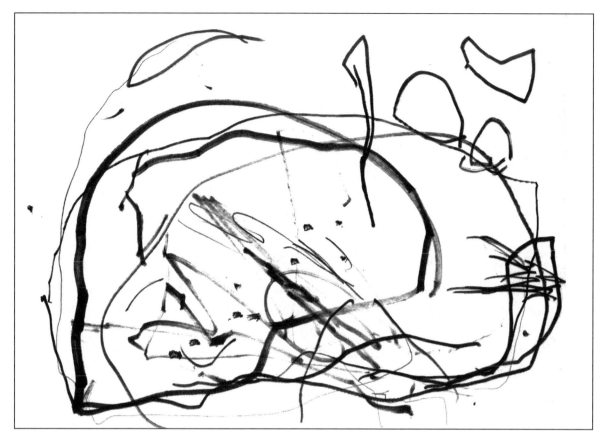

Figure 15. An arrangement of large and small outline shapes by Laurel, age 4 years, 2 months

Talking with Laurel about her drawing

It is obvious that Laurel had been working hard on ideas for shapes, their place-ment on the page, and their variations. There is a lot of drawing here! She should be congratulated on her efforts and also supported with some definite feedback.

I would simply remark on all the different kinds of things she has done. I might comment, "Look at all the different kinds of lines you've drawn here! There are some little shapes across the top and some really big circles here. They're so big they go all across the page!" If she seemed receptive, I would continue, "And inside you've made all kinds of nice squiggles and lines. You sure had some good ideas."

Of course, it is very hard to say these kinds of things the minute you are shown a complicated drawing, so take it slowly. Remember, you're talking about your child's favorite subject – herself and her ideas! Buy yourself a few initial seconds with a comment such as, "Look at this. So many different things to look at." Then try to focus on the most obvious shapes or lines that you notice and make a simple remark such as "Boy, this is a big line." You don't have to comment on everything in the drawing.

Keep in mind that even if your child likes to name her shapes, she still doesn't mean them to be pictures. As you may have done when talking about her lines, continue to keep your comments very abstract. Say, "This *shape* is large, small, or wide," or "You've used shapes [lines, patterns, dots, ideas]," rather than saying, "This looks like a bird, flower, or snail." If she meant the drawing to be a bird or a flower, let *her* tell *you*. Otherwise she will be very confused.

Suggestions for drawing games using shapes

■ Draw with your child. Since your child knows what she is doing and needs only your encouragement, drawing with her at this stage can be very helpful to you. It has probably been a long time since you drew squiggles, lines, and dots just to experiment! It would help you understand all the different decisions that she makes when she draws if you did the same.

I would suggest that you draw alongside your child, each with your own paper, unless your child wants to do a joint drawing. Tell her, "Mommy [or Daddy] is going to learn to draw some shapes and designs." If she asks why, you could say, "I have some good ideas. I want to try some, too."

■ Using figure 15 as a starting place, draw a variety of large circles within circles. Experiment with smaller odd shapes; go back and do crossovers on some of your lines. Don't be afraid to pick up ideas from your child's own drawings. Children learn a lot about drawing from watching their friends.

■ If your child asks you what you are doing, be specific. For example, you might say, "I just made a really thick line and I thought I would cross over it." If she asks why, tell her, "I wanted to see what it looks like." "Why?" "Because there's a space there," you might respond. Talking out loud about what you are doing will also help your child think about her own decision making. Try it!

Figure 16. An emphasized composition inside a border by Christopher, age 3 years, 11 months.
The piece of paper he used had a border line printed on it, which was open on the left side.
Can you see how he used this line and its opening in his drawing?

Questions & Answers

My child loves to make art at preschool, and I'm thinking about enrolling her in a Saturday class. What kind of art class would be best for her?

The best kind of class is one your daughter would enjoy. Would she prefer individual or group instruction? Let her personality be your guide in choosing a class. Would the art projects be planned for her, or would she be able to create her own? Does she like to get messy? Talk to the teacher before you register, because all classes are different.

■

My son draws very carefully at first, then suddenly scribbles all over and ruins it. Why doesn't he just draw nicely?

Your child might have some very good reasons for what he's doing! Maybe a "storm" comes along and hits his drawing. Maybe a spider eats it, or a monster stomps on it. Try asking him to explain his ideas.

■

I would like to buy some art supplies for my toddler and preschooler to share. What would you suggest?

Buy bond paper and colored paper in bulk, washable felt pens, glue sticks, and scissors. Start an art "scrap box" filled with such things as old greeting cards, labels, or bits of shiny or colored paper, and add to it often.

■

My four-year-old daughter is always naming things I can't see in her drawings. I don't know what to say to her!

Your daughter has picked up on the connection between making drawings and giving them names, but she doesn't understand yet that her drawings are also supposed to look a certain way in order for other people to understand them. This will come naturally with time. Until then, you could just say, "That's a good idea!"

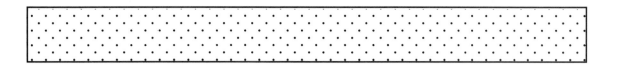

I teach three- and four-year-olds at a preschool. Do you have any suggestions for some different art projects for such holidays as Christmas or Easter? It seems as if we are always giving the children ready-made projects to color or decorate.

For a more creative slant on traditional holiday activities such as making pictures of Santa, you can begin by helping the children visualize the kinds of things that belong together for a holiday image and the shapes and colors that make them up. For example, use a picture of Santa to talk about the things that belong on his face. You might ask, Where does his face have white places? What are the white places? How many eyes does he have? Where are they? What color is his nose? Then give the children cotton balls, glue sticks, scraps of red paper and white paper, felt pens, and so forth. Let them "combine" their own version of Santa from these elements.

■

My four-year-old doesn't like to sit at a table and draw. He says he doesn't know how. What should I do to encourage him?

I wonder what he means by "drawing." Perhaps he feels he is being asked to do something he doesn't know how to do, or perhaps he feels constricted by small drawing papers. Put a length of paper on the wall of his room or a hallway, and tell him he can "decorate" it any way he wishes. You could provide a set of "smelly" markers that come in different fruit scents. If he likes action toys or superheroes, suggest he create an "action" background of shapes, scribbles, and lines for them to play in front of. In other words, try to connect drawing to his other interests, and avoid the word "drawing."

Designs

Building with lines and shapes

Children enjoy making designs with lines and shapes right through adolescence.
This drawing was done by Allison, age 12 years, 4 months

As your child becomes confident with the range of drawing skills he has developed, he will begin designing with new shapes. At first he will experiment with designing the shapes themselves, perhaps using crossover lines or lines that break up the shapes' interiors. He will become interested in how he might vary the outside edges of his shapes and how the shapes might fit together on the page. The edges of the paper themselves are seen as a large "container" for his design. Parts of his picture might interlock like pieces of a jigsaw puzzle within this container, or they might be hooked together in quite clever ways. He will begin to embellish his shapes with radiating lines or mandala-like crosses and eventually will progress to adding lines or scribbles to stand for such things as legs, arms, or hats.

In the latter part of the design stage, your child will combine *different* types of shapes to form conglomerate buildings, people, animals, or vehicles. These are accomplished with much concentration and by making many decisions. He may combine early pictures from different points of view, or use letters of the alphabet as part of his design. The possibilities for variation become tremendous, and children at this stage – ages four to six – absolutely blossom with ideas.

Be forewarned, however, that there will probably be little consistency in your child's drawings during this period. In any five-minute drawing period, he may scribble a large area in the first drawing, place his lines quite carefully in the second, draw something very tiny in each corner in the third, scribble again or add onto one of the first three drawings, and experiment with overlapping lines and shapes for the fourth one. He is also prolific: most young children don't even "warm up" until they have made four drawings in a row. Figure 17 shows 6 of 10 drawings done by one kindergarten-age boy, Samoth, in less than five minutes.

If you are looking for a clear and steady progression in your child's drawing by the time he is five or even well into his sixth year, you will probably feel quite exasperated. *Finally* your child has stopped scribbling – more or less – and "ruining" his pictures. He is obviously capable of doing better, you think. Well, not exactly! Your child has embarked on a long and wondrous journey through the world of shapes, combined shapes, designs, and "implied" pictures. Back and forth he will go from scribbles to designs for many years to come, piecing his ideas together and making sense of it all. It will help enormously if you can be patient and try to understand his thoughts and intentions as he moves through this stage.

Figure 17. Within a five-minute drawing period in his kindergarten class, Samoth, age 5 years, 5 months, made six different drawings that alternated between designs, pictures, and scribbles.

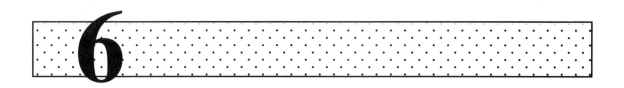

Understanding these designs

The four drawings shown in figure 18 here are called "sun" figures. Although they don't always stand for the sun and may not be drawn as clearly as a more traditional sun with rays set around a circle, they do have similar characteristics. They have each been made with one enclosed line, which is crossed over with many shorter lines. Notice how most of the spider and caterpillar "legs" are drawn right *across* the "bodies."

The drawings by Vanessa and Jenny were done when each child was four years and four months old. The fact that they were both girls and happened to be the same age is coincidental, since drawings of circles with crossover lines are made frequently between the ages of three and five.

The drawings by Paul and Matty were done when each boy was about five years old. You can see that they have a little more control over the placement of separate, carefully arranged lines that cross only the edges of the circles, not the interiors. The difference results from both their increased control of the pen and from their growing mental ability to make shorter, clearer arrangements of lines. By five years of age, both boys have an adult grip on the pen rather than the underhand fisthold that is common in younger children. In addition, each boy has a more logical and less impulsive approach to drawing. Soon they will move through this transitional stage of making designs to making early pictures, and thus begin to communicate with the outside world.

Suggestions for parents of school-age children

■ Encourage drawing designs at home if your child has begun kindergarten or elementary school. As young children start to spend more time with older children, they tend to bypass this critical developmental stage of drawing designs in favor of the next one: acquiring highly admired and easily imitated symbols like rainbows and hearts. Your child will need your support right now to maintain his interest in making designs that evolve and build on themselves.

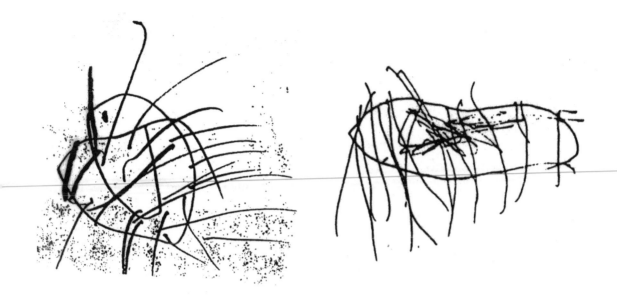

Figure 18. a "spider" by Vanessa, age 4 years, 4 months   A "caterpillar" by Jenny, age 4 years, 4 months

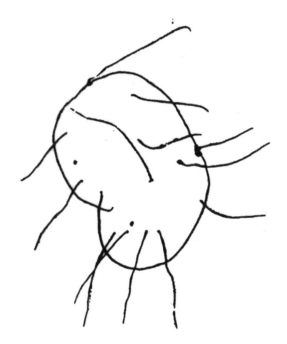

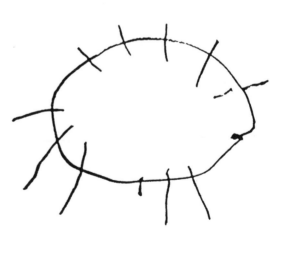

A "beetle" by Paul, age 5 years, 2 months   A "beetle" by Matty, age 5

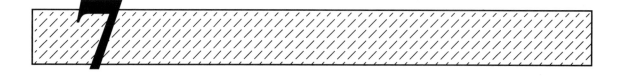

Understanding Vanessa's drawing

Figure 19 is a good example of the design stage of drawing when your child becomes more confident with her placements. Each shape is designed using "stripes," and the designed shapes themselves are fitted together on the paper like a dressmaker laying out a pattern. If you look behind the stripes, you can see outline shapes. Numerous smaller shapes are drawn both inside and outside the four larger shapes.

The placement of the crossover lines is no coincidence. Can you see how they are always at right angles to the main shape? The large shape in the bottom right corner is the most interesting. As the outline changes direction, so do the crossover lines, which always stay at right angles to the edges of the large shape.

Notice, too, the variations in the kinds of outlines Vanessa has drawn. While most of the shapes have been drawn with lines that are strong and definite, turning sharp corners when they change direction, the shape in the top right-hand corner has play-ful, curly edges. The large shape running down the left-hand side has been drawn with a gentle, wavy line. Similar variations in the edges of shapes can be seen in Jane's drawing (figure 20) and you can see how Jane has fit the pieces of her drawing together on the right-hand side.

Talking with Vanessa about her drawing

I would immediately remark on how well all the shapes fit together on the page. Vanessa has carefully planned her shapes to fill the available spaces, although neither Vanessa nor Jane have finished filling in the available background spaces. While in many cases such spaces are left for balance, it is also very common to see such an "unfinished" area in designs that otherwise fill the page. Once children can see the end of an idea, they often lose interest and may need a little encouragement to com-plete the picture. Never *insist* that a child finish a design, however. It is enough to ask, "Is this space here finished too?"

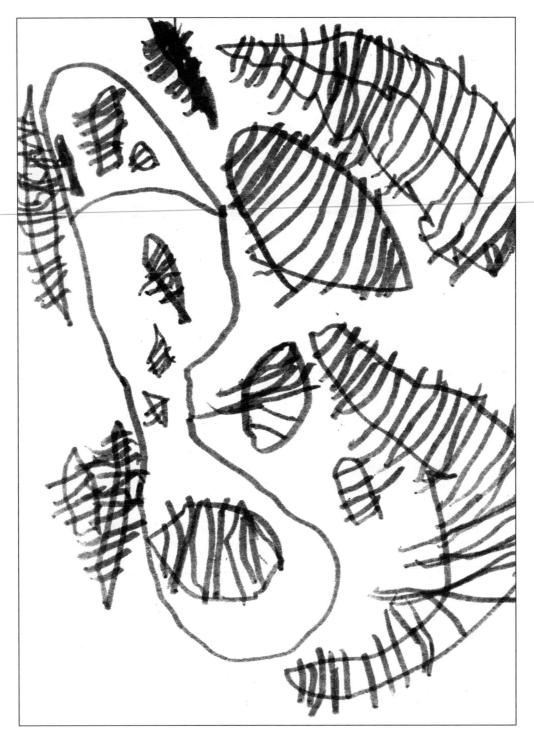

Figure 19. A complex design of crossed-over shapes by Vanessa, age 4 years, 4 months

Suggestions for drawing games using designs

If your child enjoys drawing and playing games with you, here are two ideas for shared drawings which will reinforce her new ability to place shapes. You can treat your lines and shapes as if they were real things like building blocks, mazes, or obstacle courses.

■ "Inside/Outside" is a simple game. Begin by drawing a shape such as a square or circle. Ask your child to draw the same shape *inside* yours. Add a third shape inside hers, and then ask her to draw the same shape *outside* the first one you drew. Keep working in pairs of "ins" and "outs." You will be fitting these shapes together until they are so jam-packed on the paper that there is no more room to make another shape. This game is a good lesson in coordination – (that is, controlling the pencil or pen) – following directions, and reinforcing placement.

■ In "Building Blocks," you and your child will take turns adding to a stack of squares or a necklace of circles. Begin by drawing a small square at the bottom of the page and ask your child to "balance" another square on top by drawing it. Draw a third square on top of hers, and so on. When she gets the idea, suggest that she add a *small* square, a *crooked* square, a *squashed* square and so forth. When it is your turn, ask her what kind of square you should draw. See how imaginative you can be with a simple line.

If and when your child asks you to "draw something" for her, be sure to draw *at her own level*. For example, if she is fitting simple shapes together with the odd scribbles, you should do the same. Think of the closest "equivalent" shapes for real objects, then add simple lines and scribbles for embellishments. Stop your drawing at a point where she can add on. Say, for example, "Here is a drawing of a dog, would you like to feed it? Would you like to give it a bed to sleep in?" Suggestions like these will help her learn to make decisions about where she can place shapes and scribbles in relation to the "dog," and will also make drawing a cooperative venture for the two of you.

Figure 20. An interlocking set of shapes with several kinds of edges, designed by Jane, 4 years, 11 months

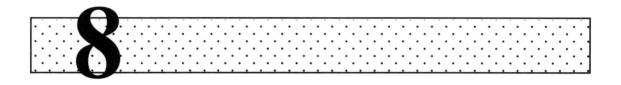

Understanding John's drawings

For several months John made designs with what appeared to be pieces of pictures. These designs were very self-assured and had a definite style. It was possible to recognize John's work out of a group of children's drawings. The recognition came partly as a result of recurring forms, which were original to John.

One of his favorite motifs was a curly cloud form, which was sometimes scribbled (figure 21) and sometimes more evenly shaped (figure 22). John seldom used it as a cloud might normally be used in a sky, however. Instead, the cloud form seemed to balance other areas that usually had straight, precisely arranged lines. In these examples, he arranged lines like building blocks to form ordinary buildings, as you can see on the right half of figure 21, or fantastic buildings, like the one perched on top of a pile of "rocks" in figure 22. This building was actually drawn from the top down.

If you compare figure 22 with figure 7 in the earlier section on scribbles, you can see how the same kinds of crossover lines have evolved another step in the developmental process of drawing.

Talking with John about his drawing

It would be difficult to guess the "meaning" of John's pictures. He didn't seem to intend any meaning; he just enjoyed the process of making his design-pictures. This can be a frustrating stage for teachers or parents who would like to find a meaning or a story in their student's or child's drawings. They look like pictures. They act like pictures. Clearly there is *something* going on!

But what your child needs at this stage is for you to accept his designs just as they are. He needs to know that it is okay, even exciting, to make pictures that don't have an obvious meaning. John would probably be very confused if he were asked "What is it?" or "Tell me about it," since as far as he is concerned he is doing a beautiful job arranging different kinds of lines – whether they are scribbled, curved, straight, or angled – in combinations that are perfectly balanced on the page. There is nothing else for him to tell!

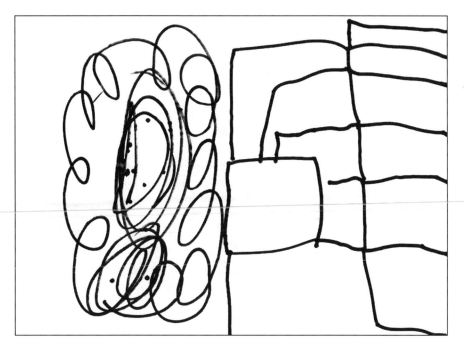

Figure 21. A dotted, curly "thing" beside a building "thing" by John,
age 4 years, 11 months

Figure 22. A design, done by John on the same day, that began at the top
and worked its way down

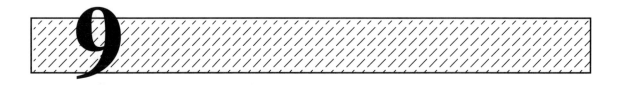

Understanding Sally's drawing

Like many four- and five-year olds, Sally was very interested in drawing the letters of the alphabet. Almost all of her drawings at this stage, which lasted for several more months, used words as part of their designs. The words were not always complete, and often some letters were missing. The letters themselves and sometimes whole words were frequently printed backwards. However, Sally was not as interested in the letters being "right" as she was in their uses for decorating her drawing. She had just discovered the alphabet. The mere *shapes* of the letters, or the ways that letters are constructed from smaller shapes and lines, were a source of fascination for her.

In figure 23, notice how well Sally fit her shapes together. All of the circles in the top half of the drawing were either elaborated with legs or rays, or filled with smaller shapes. I love the three tiny people cleverly drawn inside a jelly bean shape near the middle. (The jelly bean actually started out as a reversed letter *J*.) The large printed letters on either side of the jelly bean fill the space across the page. Smaller letters are strung in a chain across the bottom of the drawing and up the left side, like a border. Sally clearly meant the edge of the paper to be a container for her drawing.

Talking with Sally about her drawing

Some children like to talk when they draw, and some children don't. However, most children enjoy company while they draw, so don't hesitate to sit and just observe your child. As you can imagine, it was interesting to watch Sally's design evolve.

Sally was not very interested in talking to me while she drew, although she did ask me to spell out my name so she could print it on her drawing. Her attention to her drawing was very complete. When she finished, and with the exception of the group of figures in the small circle under the sun – which she identified as (clockwise from lower left) a mommy, two children, and a daddy – she said she was making "just people." Only by drawing shapes over and over and experimenting with variations on them will your child develop this sense of design.

Figure 23. A design of letters and figures used as shapes by Sally, age 4 years, 5 months

Suggestions for encouraging designs

■ If your child is starting school and learning the shapes of the alphabet and numbers, give her time and plenty of paper on which to practice. By using letters and numbers in her drawings or as part of her designs, she is continuing to develop good spatial skills.

■ Children draw best when they are quiet and thoughtful. Some children draw best after breakfast; others draw best before a bedtime story. Encourage your child to draw at the time of day and at the place (perhaps near you) when she is most calm and organized.

Questions & Answers

Our five-year-old son won't draw anything we ask him to draw, such as a sun or a person, even though all his friends can. Now he says he hates drawing. What can we do?

Your son may be unable to perform for you, especially if he hasn't figured out yet how to make designs with separate lines and shapes. Perhaps he needs more time to experiment. Buy him a 500-sheet package of bond paper and some felt pens. Tell him he can use the paper to do whatever kind of scribbling or doodling he wants.

■

Do you think it's okay for kids to put things on their drawings, such as stickers? My children always want to combine a bunch of things, instead of just drawing. Isn't this cheating?

No, it sounds very creative. Lots of children like to add stickers, then draw around them or make them look like part of the drawing. (See figure 35). Younger children may not understand that they are supposed to be making pictures that look "real" in the first place. So for them, using stickers isn't cheating at all.

■

My son never likes the pictures I put on the refrigerator, and I don't like the ones he thinks should go there. What would you do?

The problem may be that both of you have different ideas about what a picture should look like at this point. I hope this book will give you a better idea of what he's thinking, and as he gets older he will learn to understand your ideas. For now, I think young children should always be able to choose the work that goes on display and also *where* it is displayed. The refrigerator may seem like an odd place to him!

■

Why shouldn't I ask my child, "What is it?" when she draws?

In the words of one wise four-year-old, "It's not an anything – it's just a drawing." If your child doesn't mean her drawings to be about anything real, she will be very con-

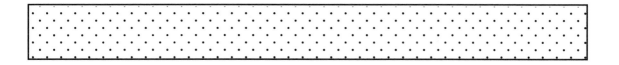

fused if she is always asked what they are. A young child may not know yet that her lines, shapes, colored places, and arrangements of scribbles are supposed to be something else as well.

■

My five-year-old never wants to color in coloring books, and when he does he can't stay inside the lines. Is this right for his age?

Remember that coloring books are an adult invention to keep children quiet and busy; they are not a source of creativity. Many children never get the point of filling in other people's pictures because they are very creative themselves. Perhaps you should ask yourself why he needs to stay inside the lines. The lines might make a good starting point for decorating or patterning the pictures instead.

■

My child draws the same shape over and over and never tries anything new. How do you explain this?

In her mind, the shape might be something different every time! As she naturally gains confidence as she grows older, you will begin to see many variations. For now, talk to her about all the things this shape might be.

Early Pictures

Representing with shapes and designs

A group of horses "floats" behind a fence, by Suzana, age 6 years, 5 months

The most striking feature of a child's early picture is the evidence of a "right way up" through either an *implied* or a *drawn* ground line. Ground lines are *implied* when all or most of the subjects in a drawing are placed so that they have obvious bottoms and tops in relation to the drawing paper. For example, if feet or legs are drawn on people, they are drawn at the bottom of people. There are no "sideways" people – unless, of course, they are meant to be doing something else besides standing or walking, such as flying, floating, or swimming. Heads or hats are similarly placed at the top of each person as well as in relation to the top of the page. This may seem very simplistic and obvious, but it is a remarkable step when children imply a ground line.

The *drawn* ground line, when it is actually drawn at the bottom of the page, is a marking that says, "This is the bottom of my picture." An early ground line could be seen in Sally's drawing (figure 23). Once your child has entered the pictorial stage, you will notice within a few months or a year that he seldom begins without drawing this ground line first. Sometimes he will even draw it at the *top* of his picture and work his way down.

Another feature of early pictures is the "bird's-eye view." For examples of this, see the drawing of the parachute game in figure 24 and also in Joshua's drawing of his family in figure 28. This view can solve many problems of composition and design.

At this stage children also create a "story" of sorts, meaning that there is more than one subject in the picture and that these subjects make sense together. For example, a drawing might show a whale and a sea; a tree and a bird; or an Easter bunny and eggs. Your child has begun to organize subjects into *types of things that go together*. However, any connections between these things, such as a common action or a cause-and-effect relationship, are probably not yet readily apparent to your child. Six-year-olds often act *on* their drawings by scribbling over them or "sliming" or "zapping" them, but in very early pictures the images are not yet doing things *to* each other.

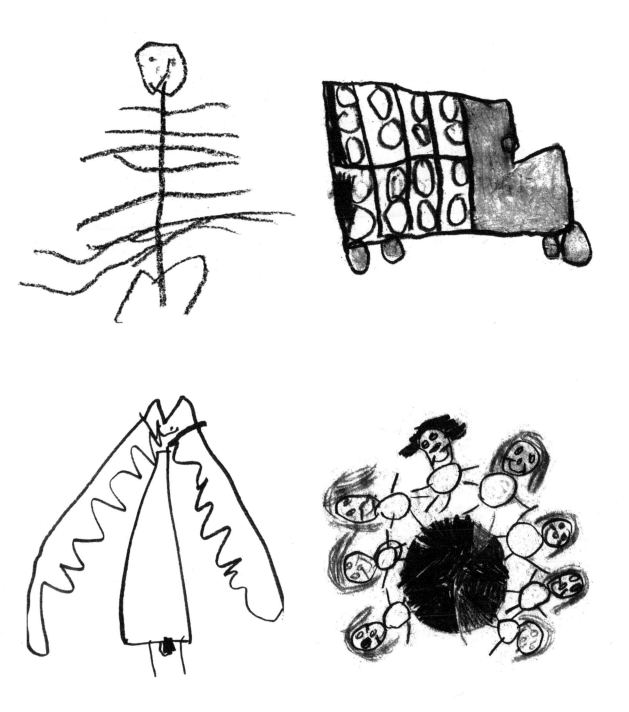

Figure 24. Five- and six-year-olds use simple shapes to design "equivalents" of real objects. Clockwise from top left: a spider, a cookie car, children playing a parachute game, and a bat.

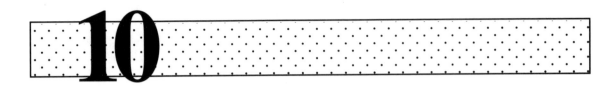

Understanding Daniel's drawing

Figure 25 is one of my favorite drawings. "Performed" by four-year-old Daniel at preschool, it is breezy, spontaneous, and uninhibited: as virtuoso as they come. It is a good example of a transitional drawing from the design stage to the early-picture stage. The combinations of shapes and lines are clearly recognized as people and various animals, and there is an implied ground line, but there is no obvious story.

Daniel drew his figures ad lib, without a plan in mind. He drew one, then another, and kept adding to them. They are drawn large or small according to how he needed them to fit into his picture.

Talking with Daniel about his drawing

How could any adult not be charmed and amused by early drawings like the one in figure 25! It is also important to comment on the variations the child is learning to make at this stage. "Look at all the different faces!" I exclaimed to Daniel. "This one's got blowy hair, and this one's got big teeth, and you made all these different shapes down the side."

Suggestions for parents of children drawing early pictures

At this stage, your child is experiencing sheer joy in repeating and varying his images. *Opportunity* to draw is the key word, and that means making a supply of drawing paper and pens easily accessible. Drawings of this sort are often the first that parents frame. Their relief that they can finally recognize something is very rewarding. But again, don't look too hard for any *meaning* here.

■ Tape a large sheet or long roll of paper low on the wall of a room or hallway. Put washable felt pens nearby. Let your child draw all over it.

■ Paint a wall or door with blackboard paint and supply chalk.

■ Rather than pointing out what "real" body parts look like, help your child create equivalent shapes for body parts using Play-Doh or a Mr. Potato Head.

Figure 25. A delightful array of figures by Daniel, age 4 years, 6 months

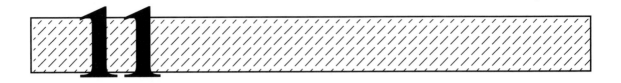

Understanding Christopher's drawing

Four-year-old Christopher had made many drawings similar to his earlier drawing (figure 16), using grouped shapes and scribbles inside borders, when he very suddenly – literally overnight – began making more representational drawings such as the one in figure 26.

As I watched one day, Christopher made four drawings in a row, all slight variations on figure 26. He began each one by drawing the head shape of the interior figure and then elaborated it with hair and facial features. Two leg lines were added next, coming directly down from the head, and were joined at the bottom to make a triangular base for each figure. Finally, each figure was carefully surrounded by a large shape. The outlines of the shapes were also elaborated in various ways, including crossover lines.

The drawing is a picture of his friend Corey inside Corey's mother. Corey's mother has "lots of hair," which Christopher has drawn using short separate lines all around the border of the "mother" shape. Notice how these crossover lines radiate from the center of the picture. The mother's head is attached to her large body shape in the top right corner.

Talking about early pictures

Like Christopher, your child at this stage will be straddling the border between reality and art, and it may happen overnight.

When he first begins to draw shapes that represent real things, he will rely on his earlier experiments with art – which meant making shapes and designs. He doesn't know anything else; they are his "stock-in-trade" so far.

As your child begins to communicate with others, he will choose shapes and designs that seem to be good *equivalents* for the shapes of real things. These early pictures are experimental and quite daring. Compliment your child on his inventiveness with shapes, spaces, and arrangements as he begins to connect with the real world.

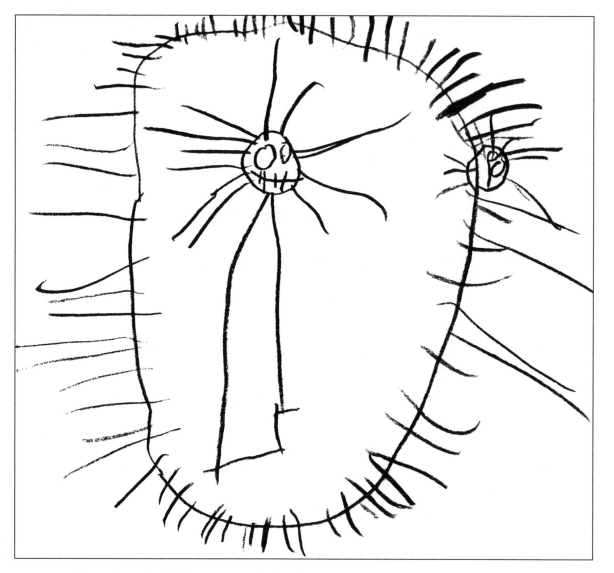

Figure 26. Christopher, age 4 years, 3 months, drew this picture of his friend inside his mother

Suggestion for combining shapes

■ Draw simple shapes with your child and talk about fitting in other shapes that might belong to them. For example, what shapes might belong inside the outline of a car, a bed, or a swimming pool?

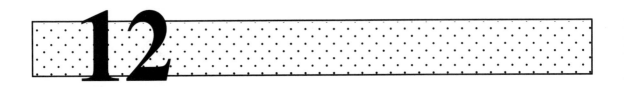

Understanding these house drawings

Figure 27 shows four outlines of house shapes, drawn by primary school children, which were filled with more shapes. Three of the drawings worked out problems of fitting door and window shapes inside the outlines. The fourth, on the bottom right, is a wonderful elaboration of many outlines within outlines.

As adults, we may feel emotions of charm, wonder, or humor when we look at them. It is important to remember that these feelings reside in us and are not intended by the children, any more than their early scribbles showed "aggression" or "chaos."

Talking about early pictures

The change from designs to recognizable images is a critical stage for many children and parents. Your child will feel bewildered if you greet images like these houses with laughter, or try to show him how things "really look." I think children are terribly clever to work out these solutions of fitting shapes into shapes on their own. Try to comment on exactly what has been done. Referring to figure 27, I might say to the children, "You've made a square that goes up to make a roof and fit in all these shapes for doors and windows. Well done!"

Suggestions for encouraging early pictures

■ Reinforce the whole picture with your comments and compliments. The houses in figure 27 were taken from larger pictures. While it is tempting to focus on such delightful details, be sure to reinforce the design skills your child uses for his *whole* picture, including scribbles, border designs, or nonrepresentational shapes.

■ Defend your child's or student's intentions against criticism from other children. Try to explain your child's drawings to others in ways that would make sense to the child himself.

Figure 27. Early pictures of houses by five- and six-year-olds which work out difficulties of fitting shapes together.

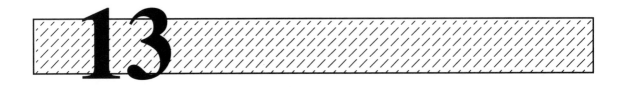

Understanding Joshua's drawing

Figure 28 is a picture of a "real" event but it is also still a design. The drawing has no ground line, includes a border, and has no particular "right way up." However, I have placed it in this section on early pictures because it clearly tells a story of sorts.

Like many four-year-olds, Joshua alternated drawing scenes like the one in figure 28 with more experimental designs or spontaneous scribbling. The subject of this drawing is his family seated around a dining table, which is covered with dishes. He began by drawing a circle in the center for the table and then attached four semicircles to the table for chairs. In the chairs are seated the four members of his family. You can imagine how hard he must have concentrated to arrange all these shapes.

At this age it is logical for Joshua, having no notion of how to draw in perspective, to draw from a bird's-eye view. This would be the most direct and efficient way to organize all the parts and include necessary details such as the delightful dishes. Notice how all of the figures have short lines attached to their hands to represent forks and knives. Around the border of the paper and therefore surrounding the group are two rows of jagged lines to "keep people out," as Joshua put it.

Talking with Joshua about his drawing

When it becomes obvious that parts of your child's drawings represent real things, I always think it is better to venture definite comments such as, "It looks like they are eating with chopsticks," rather than ask a question like, "What are those sticks in their hands?" A child who makes a complex drawing like this one has put forth a lot of effort, and it's nice to reciprocate with a little effort on your part. Your child will definitely tell you if you have guessed wrong!

Suggestions for drawing from experiences

■ Encourage your child to draw from his own experiences. His willingness to tackle complex scenes at this stage makes it easy to suggest ideas. For example, if my child

Figure 28. A picture of his family at the dinner table by Joshua, age 4 years, 5 months

and I were at the circus and he was pointing out all the action, I might respond by agreeing, "That might make a good idea for a drawing sometime. You could draw all these animals and the lights. I wonder how you could make it look noisy, though?"

■ Believing that no drawing challenge is too great for a child at this fearless stage, I would encourage many drawings of daily life, such as people lined up at the supermarket or at a crowded swimming pool. The purpose of these comments would be not only to develop new ideas for future drawings but also to show that a wide variety of subject matter can be drawn. This will help keep your child from becoming limited to symbols only.

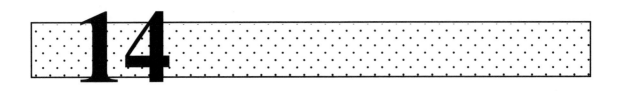

Understanding these figure drawings

These four drawings represent early figures drawn by children ages three to five. Young children draw the human body from a front view, and try to balance all the parts. Although each drawing looks different, they all share one characteristic: each is almost symmetrical, or the same on both sides.

Figure 29 is quite an advanced figure drawing, as Abigail has included the torso as well as the head and legs. However, she was not trying to draw a realistic person but rather trying to *place* her lines on the paper in a way that looked right to her. Notice how the circles for the eyes within eyes are repeated on either side of the head.

Figure 30 is what I call a "snowman" figure, as it appears to be made up of separate solid shapes drawn in the position of a figure. Figures 31 and 32 are more complicated drawings of people with embellishments added to the hands and feet. These are meant not only to stand for fingers and toes but to balance the arm and foot parts.

Talking about early figures

Your child's early figures should not be corrected. He already *know*s that our real bodies are not tubes or circles with sticks or blimps coming out of them; he simply doesn't connect these concerns about true life with his concerns about true drawings.

At this transitional stage, art is about shapes and spaces, details and elaborations, decorations and "filling in." Art is about embellishing drawings with interesting *art* details. If you can accept the necessity of six or more fingers on a hand, you will cherish your child's drawings at this stage.

Suggestion for reinforcing designs using shapes

■ The early-picture stage is excellent for any projects which allow your child to design simple rectangular spaces. Different forms of collage done on paper and arrangements of odd shapes to make pictures on felt boards are both helpful activities.

Figure 29. A symmetrical drawing of a person by Abigail, age 3 years, 6 months

Figure 30. A person made of shapes by Vanessa, age 4 years, 9 months

Figure 31. An embellished person by John, age 5 years, 2 months

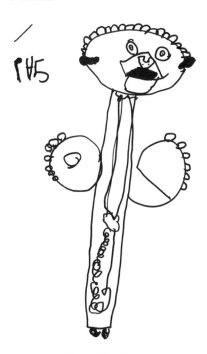

Figure 32. An embellished person by Sally, age 4 years, 6 months

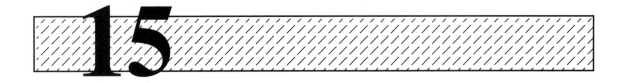

Understanding Brandon's drawing

Sometimes it is impossible to understand a drawing without having observed the child as he drew. Figure 33 is a good example of such a drawing. In figure 34, taken from the back of the same drawing, the ink from the original image shows through and we can see how Brandon began his drawing.

Brandon had just left a first-grade classroom, where the children had been busy getting ready for Easter. With thoughts of Easter foremost in his mind, he began by drawing the large egg at the top, added the Easter bunny and basket below the large egg, then embellished his scene with more figures and baskets. At this time, he became aware that his friends around him were aggressively drawing action scenes. Brandon began scribbling over his Easter picture, carefully at first, then gleefully.

Talking with Brandon about his drawing

When Brandon gave me the drawing, I asked him why he had filled it in. He told me, quite reasonably, that "the Easter bunny covered everything in slime." Of course, I take it for granted that "sliming" drawings is a perfectly ordinary thing to do in a certain age group. Right now, it is both cultural and peer-oriented. (Several years ago, everything got "zapped.") Children younger than Brandon may even completely cover a design or figure as a way of learning about "filling in." A simple observation in either case might be, "I see you filled in all your pictures."

Suggestions for parents of children who love action

■ Suggest an add-on drawing game with you or a friend. On one sheet of paper, take turns creating one drawing, which you make up as you go along. Use your imaginations to think up subjects and actions, change the subjects into something else, or perhaps put people in a "fix" and then "save" them.

■ Be sure to keep your own drawing at his level. If your child still scribbles sometimes, make some of your shapes with scribbles, too.

Figure 33. A "slimed" drawing by Brandon, age 6 years, 1 month

Figure 34. The same drawing before it was "slimed."

Questions & Answers

Every single picture our five-year-old daughter draws has a heart, a sun, a rainbow, and a little girl in it. Should we encourage her?

Of course. She is showing you that she knows how to draw things in a way that you will understand. You can praise her for communicating with you rather than for the actual things she draws. Also, read ahead to the advice on talking about symbols on pages 84 and 85.

■

My daughter never colors anything the right color. She might start to make her sky blue, then she changes to yellow, and then finishes with another color. Should I be concerned?

No. Sometimes children start off with good intentions, but things just get boring. A sky can be an awful lot of paper to color. Actually, a three-colored sky sounds very nice!

■

My six-year-old draws things much bigger or smaller than they really are. Should I tell him, or will I hurt his feelings?

Tell your child that some people believe pictures should look like things in real life, and that when he is older he will understand these people better. But there's no good reason why things should have to look real in drawings. After all, a drawing isn't real.

■

Our daughter, who is five, draws things so you can see what's inside them. Is this unusual?

Not at all. It's quite logical for most children at a certain stage. Right now she is in the business of giving out information when she draws, and this is more important than making things look real. Her "X-ray" drawings are a very clever way to show the information inside a larger shape.

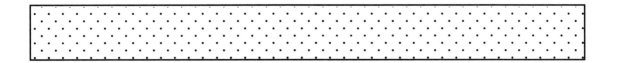

My son is seven and still draws in only one corner of the paper. Is this okay?

It's very unusual. If he is starting to draw designs or early pictures and still stays in one corner, he may be feeling anxious about other people seeing them. Or he may be worried that his pictures will be displayed when they are finished. If this is the case, tell him he can keep them "secret" after he's done.

■

My eight-year-old son criticizes my six-year-old daughter because she "can't draw." What can I tell him?

Ask him what he thinks drawing is. Then tell him that a person's definition of drawing changes all the time, especially as a person gets older.

■

My seven-year-old draws things on their side and even upside down. Why does he do this?

The process of coming to understand drawings as a "window to a view of the world," in which everything is right side up, in proportion, and looks real, is a long one. It also involves thinking about what is and is not "real." Many adult artists never make this choice, because they don't believe drawings necessarily have to look like a view of the real world! Your child will make up his own mind in time as he observes others drawing.

Scenes

Interpreting our world

A design combining a boat on the open sea with a sky full of balloons by Julian, age 8 years, 11 months

As children grow, they become comfortable with the fundamentals of making a picture. They have an intuitive sense of both "right way up" and ground lines. They are able to express their ideas through simple but concrete images, such as animals and people, and combine them with environmental images, such as buildings or landscapes. Most of their drawings will combine two or more subjects and show an implied action between them. For example, rain falls on people, an animal chases another animal, or a man hides in a house. Through their drawings, they are now telling stories of sorts in scenes that begin to interpret our world.

This is a very dynamic stage of children's art which will last as long as your child draws spontaneously and remains uncritical of his drawing skills. He is truly the master of his own imagination at this point.

His imagination is capable of communicating almost anything: his fantasies, images seen on television, versions of stories and legends told to him, action and movement, and images drawn from real life. While he will still start his drawings impulsively, he is more capable of organizing and planning his scenes as he draws, as Ryan did in figure 36. You will soon notice finer detail in areas where he begins to display his personal ideas about such concepts as humor, beauty, or ugliness. Your child may also add creative components such as the butterfly stickers Jessica added to her drawing in figure 35.

This is a critical stage for reinforcing his design skills as the underpinnings of his artwork. Not only is purely abstract designing extremely enjoyable right through adulthood, but every picture or scene needs to have a visible or invisible underpinning of design to hold the picture together as a whole. The examples of children's art in this section show a typical progression in your child's pictorial development as he learns to combine pictures that represent real or imagined subjects together in what is still essentially a design.

Figure 37 combines obvious design features (rows of lines or "stripes") equally with pictorial images. In figure 38, we see a well-balanced symbolic drawing by a six-year-old. Figure 39 shows implied action: the various images face one another to interact and are pleasingly spaced on the page. Figure 40 again contains a set of recognizable symbols, nicely balanced and organized, by an almost eight-year-old girl who is ready for more realistic approaches. These approaches may include choosing a more interesting point of view; learning to overlap or partially "hide" her subjects;

Figure 35. A self-portrait of Jessica, age 5 years, 10 months, pushing her doll carriage.
She added butterfly stickers to her drawing.

or developing backgrounds, patterns, and actions more fully. This strongly representational stage of drawing literally "sets the scene" for your child's drawing development in later years.

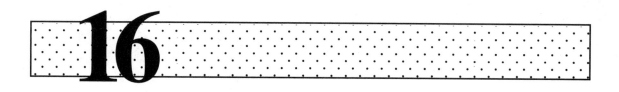

Understanding Ryan's drawing

Spring had come to the neighborhood, and spring themes were being played out in the schools. Five-year-old Ryan "collected" eleven different images of the season all in one picture (figure 36).

What is remarkable about this drawing is the great *variety* of shapes that make up the animals and other images. While ovals are the main shapes used for bodies, look at how Ryan has varied the ovals *and* the head shapes. Even the cow head at the top left and the rabbit head at the bottom right, both of which appear similar at first glance, have definite variations (the cow's head indents at the jaw line while the rabbit's jaw is round) and different internal markings (the tops of the cow's ears are marked with lines while the insides of the rabbit's ears are marked with dark spots).

Notice too, the beginning of a definite scene. There is a ground line at the bottom, colored in solidly, with a tree and a flower growing out of the ground. A bird rests on the top of the tree, and a cloud hangs in the sky above. The rabbit on the right walks on the ground, balancing a basket of eggs on his head.

However, from this point on the picture is pure fantasy. A row of smaller figures runs diagonally from the bottom left to the top right, and the large cow is drawn in the "sky" area to balance the large rabbit in the opposite corner.

Talking with Ryan about his drawing

I would compliment Ryan on all the variations in his animal forms by first pointing out the different body shapes: some are round, some long, others narrow or tall. I would add, "The branches on the tree are really good." His animals are so delightful, so clear and precise, that I would suggest lots of ideas for future drawing.

Suggestions for more animal pictures

Drawing different animals gives your child a good opportunity to think about all kinds of shapes. Here are some suggestions:

Figure 36. An assortment of Spring animals by Ryan, age 5 years, 8 months

■ Draw four different animal masks.

■ Tell a story in a drawing about a problem that some animals face and solve.

■ Fold and staple some paper to make a book about an animal with a bright idea.

■ Check toy or stationery stores for kits that let you design an animal picture for a dinner plate.

■ Draw an animal on a T-shirt with neon puff-paints.

■ Compose animals by arranging geometric or odd shapes on a felt board.

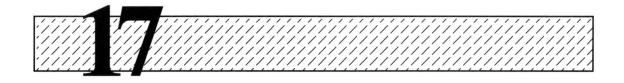

Understanding Megan's drawing

Figure 37 is one of my favorite drawings because of the way everything is balanced. Megan has repeated the same kinds of lines in different ways to create feelings of energy and movement. For example, the row of horizontal lines behind the bunny is repeated, using shorter lengths, down the right-hand side of the picture. The slightly diagonal tilt of the lines behind the bunny, his pointed toes, and his splayed fingers, make him appear to rise or fly. There is a sense of harmony and happiness throughout the picture.

Talking with Megan about her drawing

Once children begin to relate different subjects and designs, there is bound to be a story of sorts implied in their drawings. Sometimes this story makes sense as a series of actions and sometimes it doesn't. The important thing for an interested adult to remember is to *slow down* and talk about the areas one at a time. Saying to a child, "Tell me about this drawing" is really asking for too much information all at once.

Although I love Megan's drawing for its design of lines and shapes, I was curious to know more about what she was thinking when she drew it. I asked her, "Who is in the picture?" and she told me, "The Easter bunny."

"Ah, and this is his egg down here?" I asked.

"Yes, and that's the rainbow," she replied, pointing to the curved lines above the rabbit.

"I really like all these lines," I then told her, running my hand up and down the two horizontal rows. "What is he doing?"

"He's trying to climb up a rock. It's like a ladder."

"Ah," I replied again. "And what will he do there?"

"He wants to sit on the rainbow," she informed me, very matter-of-factly, and left.

Your child may, of course, not be in the mood for such a detailed conversation with every drawing she does. Start with one or two simple questions, and if your interest is genuine, you will usually be able to learn a little.

Figure 37. The Easter bunny climbs to the rainbow by Megan, age 7 years, 1 month

Suggestion for using scenes in a story

■ When children between the ages of six and eight draw pictures that have action or a series of events, they can make a storybook or a cartoon strip. First, discuss a possible subject and the events that might happen. Then divide a large piece of paper into four squares. Your child can draw four stages in the story development, one in each square.

The finished drawings can be left intact or cut into four pieces and stapled together to make a book. Since this is quite a complex project, help your child plan it out and encourage her to include lots of details.

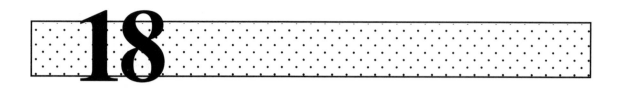

Understanding Kristine's drawing

In figure 38, six-year-old Kristine has created a well-balanced design using a roller-skating cat, a ground line, and several separate symbols that she has collected on her paper to fill in the sky area and to decorate the cat.

Once your child begins school and is constantly exposed to the artwork of other children, you will notice the appearance of many symbols in her drawings. The symbols appear to be chosen from a child's list of things that are good and acceptable in a drawing and that are easy to imitate. Most girls ages six and seven regularly include stars, balloons, clouds, rainbows, hearts, and suns in their pictures, so your child will be in good company – which of course is the point. Your child is quickly learning that these symbols make her drawings acceptable to other children, who recognize them and can copy them, too.

In spontaneous drawings, some symbols may actually be quite useful as a kind of shorthand. For example, handy stick figures may be used to quickly indicate figures in an action scene (see page 155), or V-shaped birds may add a nice area of balance or emphasis – in the same way that dots once did – in a landscape scene.

Whether the use of symbols is "good" or "bad" really depends on the drawing. However, if you find your child is limiting herself by using only symbols, she may need encouragement from you to continue with her own good ideas.

Talking with Kristine about her drawing

When I talk to children who use a lot of common symbols, I try to help them distinguish between real life and what I see as an early cartoon form. I might ask Kristine, "Don't you wish you could *really* see the sun, a rainbow, and some clouds all at the same time in the sky? Drawing is nice because you can put things like that together," or "Don't you wish you could really see a cat roller skating? I wonder if it would have hearts drawn on the sides like yours does."

Figure 38. A pussycat goes roller skating by Kristine, age 6 years, 1 month

Suggestion for using symbols in scenes

■ Rather than disallowing symbols, which are important at this age for peer acceptance, try to suggest a creative use of them so that children don't take them for granted. Encourage your child to use her imagination. Ask her, for example, what would be a really good way to use a rainbow. Could it come out after the rain? If so, how would she make everything look wet? How could she use a heart symbol in a drawing? Could it be a house, a lake, or the opening of a tunnel? And if the sun put sunlight all over everything in the picture, what would that look like? Your child could use different colors or different types of lines to show sunlight.

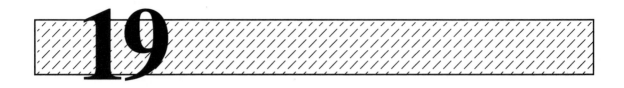

Understanding Cheehan's drawing

Six-and-a-half-year-old Cheehan demonstrated not only pictorial realism but a sense of humor in his undersea scene (figure 39), which he began by drawing a waterline along the top.

As Cheehan put it, the man in the cage is "safe from the sharks," an image he may have seen on television. The man is crossed over with lines that denote bars on the front *and* on the back of the cage. Most children like to draw bars for cages on top of captive subjects. Cheehan took this one step further and ensured that the back of the man is also protected – by drawing from the front, which is all he knows for now. The man in the cage is carefully joined by an air supply to the boat, which was drawn above the water. The hose containing the air supply is (logically) drawn as an extension from the man's head. Surrounding the cage in a balanced semicircle are several kinds of fish and a crab. Cheehan shows an awareness of the underpinnings of design by positioning the two larger fish on the left and the crab at the bottom so that each one faces the man, even at an angle, much the same way that Christopher radiated the "hair" lines in figure 26. This subtlety makes the animals part of the same picture, or story. When he was almost finished with his drawing, Cheehan decided to have them play baseball. The crab catches the ball while one of the smaller fish holds a tiny black bat, wears a baseball cap, and "stands" on a mound. The idea began when Cheehan decided that the crab's claws looked too much like baseball mitts.

Talking with Cheehan about his drawing

Cheehan was more than happy to talk about his drawings with me. It didn't seem to matter to him whether he talked while he was drawing or after he was finished. Like many six-year-olds, he was at a stage where he was confident with his ability to depict scenes and action, and he was very interested in communicating a "narrative" or story in his work. He was also flexible about changing the direction or content of his story as he worked. If your child is at this stage, you will both enjoy a conversation about the content of his picture, while it is in progress or afterward.

Figure 39. Man in a sharkproof cage with baseball-playing fish and crab by Cheehan, age 6 years, 6 months

Suggestions for imagining unusual views

Capitalize on your child's imagination and sense of humor by offering suggestions for creative drawings from an unusual point of view, such as:

■ What his brother keeps under his bed or in his closet.

■ What he dreams about.

■ What his bicycle wheels have seen.

■ What's in the ground underneath your house.

In addition, you can tell or read short stories to your child and have him illustrate them as you read.

Understanding Jennifer's drawing

Figure 40, in contrast with figure 33, is a drawing most people would understand. The lines are drawn clearly, and the subjects are immediately recognized. It contains many approved subjects, such as the sun, the tulip, and the balloons. The border surrounding her artwork, which was Jennifer's own idea and the starting point for this drawing, provide an added appeal and a finished look.

Between the ages of seven and nine, your child might become quite self-conscious about drawing and say she "can't draw." If she has been using a lot of symbols in her drawing, as Jennifer did in figure 40, she might also become a little bored with drawing. While Jennifer used cultural symbols that made her picture easy to understand, such as the sunglasses on the sun, the balloons held by the girl, and the two leaves at the base of the tulip, she might have gone on to add more personal details that would communicate more of her own ideas. Patterns, textures, words, or letters, all used by Charlene in figure 41, give drawings an added sparkle. However, your child might be at a stage when it isn't easy for her to do this without help.

Talking with Jennifer about her drawing

By the age of seven or eight, children are ready to move out of the symbolic stage if they receive the right kind of encouragement. Unfortunately, many adults have never progressed beyond this point themselves, so they find it difficult to know what to say. *Without* the right kind of encouragement, many children will stop drawing altogether.

When I talk with older children about drawings that contain a lot of symbols, I try to emphasize what makes their drawings unique. "I like the border around your drawing," I might say to Jennifer. "You've done a nice job of arranging things inside it." I would also look for ways that common subject matter might be drawn a little differently. "What is this flower or tree on the right side? I like that. And her skirt looks transparent. Is it supposed to be? No? Maybe that's an idea you could use another time, because you can see how well it works."

Figure 40. A simple scene by Jennifer, age 7 years, 11 months

Suggestions for parents of children who begin to lose interest in drawing

During the middle years, parents and teachers will have to begin working very hard to emphasize both the more realistic and the more imaginative features of children's drawings. Here are many ideas that may help at this awkward stage.

■ Ask your child to draw from different viewpoints. For example, can she figure out how to draw a person from the side instead of from the front? How can she draw a scene like the one in figure 40 from above and show the tops of things?

■ Encourage your child to overlap parts of her drawing. Talk about things that are "hiding" behind other things, and suggest that she draw the objects in front first.

■ Suggest that your child draw a background for a scene, then draw all its subjects on a separate sheet of paper. She can cut them out and "compose" them on the background. Talk with her about where and how to place or overlap the pieces, then glue them in place.

■ By the age of six or seven, your child may be exhausting her own ideas for drawing with simple shapes and symbols. You can refuel her imagination by looking through biology and botany books to find ideas for patterns and shapes. Also look for patterns and textures in slides through a microscope. Encourage your child to study patterns and colors in nature to increase her drawing "vocabulary."

■ Suggest drawing something for every letter of the alphabet. Ask your child to draw an object in your house for each of the twenty-six letters. You can start with an apple, a box, and a coat hanger, for example. How about making up something silly and imaginary for each letter, too, like *applepus* combining an apple and an octopus, or *Beetlejuice*? Stretch the limits of your imagination and design skills.

■ Play memory games with patterns: look, memorize, conceal, and draw from memory a pattern found on clothes, sheets, or upholstery in your house. Then think of something real or imaginary that your child could draw using that pattern.

■ Encourage your child to relate the parts of her drawing to one another. Ask, "What is one thing *doing* to another?" How can she show this in her drawing?

■ Encourage the narrative or story-telling element. Children this age need lots of opportunities to develop scenes of action and to show important moments in events.

Figure 41. A scene showing the use of overlapping and patterning by Charlene, age 9 years, 11 months

Questions & Answers

When our five-year-old son draws people, they all look exactly the same. Should I say something to him?

Your son won't make people in his drawings look different until the connection between real people and drawings of people becomes important to him. When this happens, he will start to single out the bits and pieces that make different people memorable to him. For one it may be a moustache, for another it may be big boots or high heels, and for another it may be an accessory such as a brooch or a cane. Not until adolescence do children always discriminate finer differences between people, such as the size of body parts or such details as noses.

■

My six-year-old daughter draws a line along the bottom of her paper and then doesn't know what else to draw. How can I help her?

She may feel that something particular, such as a scene, is expected of her. Remind your daughter that her drawings show her own good ideas, and they don't have to be pictures other people will understand. Also, if her paper is too large, it may be intimidating for her. In this case, help her plan her ideas out loud before she draws.

■

Our seven-year-old son draws himself bigger than anything else in the picture, including his father. What does this mean?

It means that he doesn't connect the real sizes of people to his drawings yet. This is quite normal.

■

I was thinking about buying some different art materials for my child. What would you suggest for a five-year-old who likes to draw?

At this age, so many things are connected to a child's interest in drawing. For example, dress-up clothes encourage a child to act out his fantasies. Construction toys such as Lego or Duplo help a child plan and develop ideas. Materials for construction

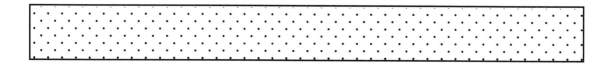

or collage, such as balsa wood, pieces of cellophane and scrap paper, or recycled industrial materials, help a child take chances and be creative as well as manipulate and adjust his ideas as they develop. Specific materials for drawing that may capture your child's fancy are sidewalk chalk, bathtub crayons, or colored sand for sand "paintings."

■

My seven-year-old son only draws "good guys" and "bad guys" and so do his friends. Is this because they watch too much TV?

Between the ages of five and seven, children are very interested in definite opposites. In other words, they see the world and the things in it as black or white, nice or mean, good or bad. Most TV shows for this age group cater to this type of evaluation. Whether or not they are watching too much TV, TV is watching them! Your child's drawings will naturally reflect his interest in opposing themes until he begins to see the world as more varied and complex.

■

Our six-year-old talks the whole time she's drawing, but she doesn't draw very much.

For young children, a drawing is something that "happens" mainly in their thoughts and feelings, rather than on paper. They may be verbalizing what is going on in their heads even though their drawings often show little evidence of "the real story." This is why it is so important (and so interesting) to sit with young children and listen or talk with them while they draw.

Separate Objects

Learning to compose

A collection of separate objects by Jennifer, age 7 years, 11 months

Your child's middle years might be quite a dull period for creativity and originality in contrast to the imagination she showed in her drawings before the age of seven. Since she was capable of composing an entire scene only recently, this new stage can be confusing to her as well as to parents and teachers. But as your child develops more realistic approaches to drawing, it is important to understand she might plateau or even regress for a period.

One of the most difficult stages for your child is what I call the separate-object phase. In this phase, individual images – whether they are drawn realistically, symbolically, or a combination of both – are not connected. These unconnected drawings can appear at any time in your seven- to nine-year-old's representational development and reappear at any time in later years when she loses confidence in her drawing ability.

The phase affects children who are concerned with precision and prefer their drawings neat and uncluttered. Your child's lack of confidence in coordinating her ideas may also be complicated by a growing self-consciousness about whether her drawings are "right" or "good." Many girls feel very sensitive during this period and may be cautious about taking creative chances. Perhaps the dynamic possibilities of portraying action delays this phase for most boys.

Drawings of separate objects appear to lack purpose, since they show a collection of images that don't seem to share any relationships. Your child may revert to just making patterns with a few repeated images that feel comfortable, such as the trees in figure 42. Or her objects may be set in a composition but too widely spaced because she lacks information about what to do for her background.

She may also have limited experience in connecting her subjects to one another as well as to the background. In other words, she may *demand* more of her drawings at this time than her earlier design experience can provide.

Whether she is making realistic pictures or imaginary pictures, if your child is having trouble connecting separate images, this chapter will help you to help her. You can talk about planning ahead and trying to visualize all the parts. You can encourage her to look at patterns, textures, and shapes in nature so she will have a wider drawing vocabulary for making marks and designs.

By the age of 10, she is also old enough to start thinking about how things "really" look and how they should affect one another in a drawing, as the bridge and trees

Figure 42. A bridge over a forest by Elizabeth, 12 years, 1 month. Because the trees do not become smaller in the distance as the bridge does, they do not seem like part of the same drawing.

affect each other in figure 42. Above all, she needs to look closely at the *reasons* for her drawings, and make her purposes clear. Laura's situation in figures 46–48 is a good example of how clear goals can give your child extra confidence.

Understanding Rachael's drawing

What a combination of subjects and styles is shown in figure 43! Rachael began with the feathery baby chick inside the egg or nest at the bottom of the drawing, then stopped drawing for several minutes. She continued with the very definite curved line at the top of the drawing which forms a set of three hills. She added decorative lines for the clouds and sky and detailed two of the hills a little. Again she stopped drawing, and there was a long wait before she suddenly drew the girl and the cat, then the two large trees and two small Easter eggs – all within and below the curve of the middle hill – in quite a different style and pen pressure. She finished by filling in the remaining space with the raindrop pattern.

Talking with Rachael about her drawing

Clearly unsure about the rightness of her choices while she drew this picture, Rachael, and other children at an indecisive stage, would benefit from a great deal of support and some planning ahead. Since Rachael had so many ideas to choose from in figure 43, she could use this drawing as the basis for making another drawing or two. I would simply point out all the separate things in it, and talk with her about different combinations for new pictures.

Suggestions for helping children who draw "busy" pictures

■ Help your child organize her thoughts and gain confidence by visualizing scenes *before* she draws them. You can talk about the main subjects ("Who's going to be in the picture?") and their actions ("What are they going to be doing?"). Help her imagine the spacing of her subjects with questions like "Are they going to be in the middle of the picture or the bottom?" and "What's beside them?" Once a few of the basics are planned in advance, your child will have more freedom to embellish and detail her ideas.

■ Try reading a story description or a short fable, then suggest that your child illustrate it. Before she begins, help her list the subjects and details she wants to include.

Figure 43. A combination of different subjects and styles by Rachael, age 7 years, 1 month

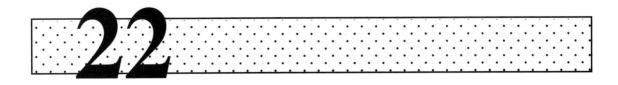

Understanding Kerry Ann's drawing

Kerry Ann is an eight-year-old girl who is becoming quite skilled at drawing many subjects realistically. In figure 44, she illustrated the texture of the four ice cream cones at the bottom and drew a pattern of drips on the three ice cream cones at the top of the picture. Like Vanessa in figure 19 and Jane in figure 20, she fit her ice cream cones together on the paper in an interlocking pattern. The background space and the space taken up by the cones are well balanced.

You can see that Kerry Ann has developed an ability for realism which is parallel to her understanding and use of design. The two things are equal, as they should be by the age of eight. She is now ready to go beyond the simple element of *arrangement* in her designs and to provide some kind of action or relationship between the parts. In other words, it is time for her to add some "verbs" to her "nouns"!

Talking with Kerry Ann about her drawing

Kerry Ann drew the picture with a pencil first, then traced over it with a felt pen, which can be a good planning technique. She could now put a clean piece of paper over this drawing and use it as a guide for drawing it again. At the same time she could think about what the ice cream cones might be doing, or what they could do, to connect better to each other and to the background, as well as to create some action. For example, she might try drawing some drips, melting puddles, or shadows cast from the cones onto the background.

Suggestions for parents of self-conscious drawers

If your child has trouble thinking of drawing ideas, here are some suggestions which would also make good gifts:
■ Have your child do a drawing or painting to tape on the back of your aquarium to give the fish or turtles a new "outlook." It can be laminated for protection against moisture.

Figure 44. A design of ice cream cones by Kerry Ann, age 8 years, 9 months

■ Draw a family portrait using snapshots for reference. Think about what to draw in the background *first*.

■ Draw a "portrait" of your home or a relative's home. Think about how the house is joined to the yard. Are there stairs and a walkway? Bushes or trees overlapping the house? Telephone poles or neighboring houses behind the house?

■ Try drawing a portrait of the family pet with all of her or his favorite things around him. Think about what the walls look like behind your pet's bed.

■ Make a family "totem pole" design that includes the family pets. Think about ideas for joining the figures to one another and making everything symmetrical.

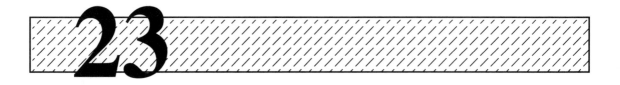

Understanding Erica's drawing

Figure 45 is a very pleasing design. Eight-year-old Erica began by breaking up her paper into foreground and background parts that are fairly symmetrical. Notice how the two hills that partially overlap the rising sun balance each other, as do the trees below them.

Although the smaller images of the animals are not placed symmetrically in the picture, they also balance each other. If you cover any of the animals or the spotted bush on the bottom left with your hand, you can quickly see how each one adds an important visual weight to the picture.

At first glance this drawing appears quite graphic and flat. However, Erica has used some realistic overlapping, which is appropriate for her age. For example, both trees overlap the hills behind them; the spotted bush overlaps the tree; and the bunny overlaps the hills. This ability to overlap subjects in a drawing comes relatively late in your child's development, and it is an important milestone. It shows that she is beginning to understand and use the real appearance of the world in her drawings.

Talking with Erica about her drawing

I would encourage Erica to help the animals "connect" by asking her, "Where do you think this bunny came from? Can you show that? How would you do that?" She might try drawing some footprints, pathways, or marks that show jumping action. I could also ask, "What are these animals walking on?" Erica could consider drawing marks for grass, pebbles, or bumps.

Sometimes children just need a little encouragement to take chances by trying out marks they may not have tried before. Encourage your child to visually express different feelings of *sensation*. If your child is drawing an outdoor scene, you might ask, "How do you think the ground feels beneath your feet?" "Imagine yourself walking through this picture. Do you feel something rough or soft? Wet or dry? Is the ground cold or warm?" Tell your child that there is really no "right" way to draw the ground, but it might be fun to try out different kinds of marks!

Figure 45. A designed scene by Erica, age 8 years, 10 months

Suggestions for textures and patterns

■ Your child might be interested in looking at a Letraset catalog for different textures and patterns used by graphic artists to represent nature. She could copy some of the patterns to get new ideas for textures in her drawings.

■ Walk barefoot outside with your child and describe the ground as you walk. How does it feel on your feet? Talk about how she might draw it.

■ Look at illustrated manuscripts, Persian miniature paintings, and china dishes for patterning ideas to use in drawings.

Understanding Laura's drawing

Older children frequently change paper midway through their drawings, as opposed to much younger children who like to "knock off" a rapid series of finished ideas. Thirteen-year-old Laura had drawn four similar pictures of a cat, each one an improvement on the last, before she suddenly switched to the landscape idea shown in figures 46 through 48.

Like many adult artists, Laura used the technique of developing her ideas through a series of sketches or studies. It was as if by sketching out her thoughts as they came, an idea would appear. This is an excellent approach for getting warmed up, but one which may also end with a series of separate objects on the page. When this occurs, the group of objects often *looks* somewhat like a picture (figure 47), and the child, confused, stops drawing.

Talking with Laura about her drawings

It is important for parents and teachers to help older children occasionally move beyond their studies to finished pictures. When I saw figure 47 I suggested to Laura, "Good, you've got a lot of different things to work with in all these drawings. You've got the cat drawings you did earlier, and here you've got a building, a tree, trees in the distance on a mountain, a stump. . . . You're probably going to have to narrow down your choices a little, because they may not all fit in the same drawing."

Laura also needed some guidance in determining a *purpose* for her drawing. I said, "Maybe the first thing to decide is, do you want a long view of scenery from a distance, or do you want a closeup of something?" She opted for a long view, and I again turned to her drawings in figures 46 and 47 for reinforcement. "You've got some nice line textures in your tree (figure 46) and in the ground under the stump (figure 47). Think about all the different ways that lines can go when you draw your landscape," I said. In less than three minutes, she was back with the dynamic landscape sketch in figure 48; she only needed to think ahead a little.

Figure 46. Unrelated objects by Laura, age 13 years, 2 months

Figure 47. The beginning of a scene by Laura, on the same day.

Suggestions for planning realistic compositions

■ Show your child how to use photocopiers to help plan compositions. A copier that enlarges and reduces can be a wonderful aid for composing a drawing or painting from separate studies or from sketchbook pictures.

Your child can copy her favorite images several times, both larger and smaller than the original, then cut them out and arrange them on a piece of paper.

Is something too big or too small? Help her choose different-sized images until the pictures work together. She can move them around and overlap them in different ways, trying the same image in the foreground and in the background of the picture.

The finished assemblage can be used as a guide for composing a picture. She could complete the drawing or painting with patterns and textures between the components.

■ Help your child understand how to show distance in a picture. After choosing a theme such as a scene or landscape, she can cut out pictures of different subjects – trees, buildings, or cars, for example – from a magazine.

Help her compare the sizes of the pictures to one another. Point out how a car picture may be larger than a building picture, or how a person may be taller than a tree.

The individual pictures can then be arranged on a piece of paper according to size. Show your child how the car picture, which may be disproportionately larger than the building, will be placed low on the page to show it is closest to us, while the building will be placed higher on the page to show it is in the distance. You can also suggest that she overlap different objects.

On a separate piece of paper, have your child make a drawing of her final arrangement. Have her *begin by drawing the objects that are lowest on the page*, then add other things that are partially hidden behind them and higher on the paper to show distance.

■ Provide sketchbooks for regular doodling. Sometimes your child will welcome talking things over, and other times she will just be making "bored" drawings. It is important for her to be able to do the "bored" drawings, too. These are like doodles that have no obvious purpose or intent; as her thoughts meander from subject to subject, so do her drawings. By the age of 10, your child should be provided with a new sketchbook at regular intervals for what parents and teachers might perceive as "meaningless," personal, or "bored" drawings.

Figure 48. A well-organized landscape drawing by Laura

Questions & Answers

When my seven-year-old paints, she doesn't want to "blend" her colors or let them run together as in real paintings. She gets angry if I try to show her how.

At some stage, most children resist letting their colors "touch" one another. It sounds as if your daughter is still treating paint the way she would felt pens or crayons; that is, using paint to draw lines and to color in areas. As she spends more time painting, she will gradually discover what paint can do that is different from felt pens or crayons.

■

My child, who is nine, loves to draw and paint, but she has never won a contest. How can I help her improve?

This is very hard question, because I think the idea of art contests is terrible. Art is about expressing your own thoughts and ideas, experimenting with new approaches, and trying to match the feelings inside you with your art. How can these intentions be judged in a way that is helpful to a child? Certainly not through contests! You can help your child improve by reaffirming that her art belongs to her.

■

My seven-year-old son always asks me to draw things for him, but I can't draw. What should I tell him?

Tell him you will try to help. For example, if he wants to draw a "real" horse, tell him you and he should think about it together first. Talk about the kinds of shapes that might make up a horse, the number of legs and ears a horse has and how long or big they are, and the things that make a horse look like a horse and not a dog – such as a mane. You will find more detailed information on discussing shapes in my book *Teach Your Child to Draw* (Lowell House, 1990).

■

My eight-year-old daughter spends hours putting every tiny little detail in her drawings, but she will only draw "girls" and their hairdos and dresses.

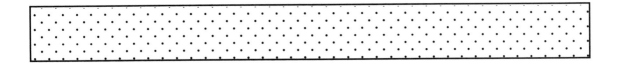

By repeating images over and over, children not only claim them as their own but learn to fine-tune the details. Remember, too, that she is still young and may not have been exposed to a lot of other choices or ideas yet.

■

I think my 11-year-old son's drawings look stiff. Should I tell him?

Because older children become very interested in details, they often lose sight of the whole picture. Take the emphasis off the details by pointing out where he has connected different things to one another in his pictures, perhaps by overlapping different parts, by repeating patterns or textures, or by creating a sense of "story" or action.

■

My 10-year-old daughter is always critical of her drawings and paintings. She never has a nice word to say about them. I think they're pretty good, but I wish she would stop complaining and putting herself down. Do you have any suggestions?

This sounds pretty normal for her age group, and it probably affects everything she does, not just drawing! It sounds like she just needs reassurance that the appearance of her drawings is not everything. You can talk to her about the experiences and events she draws upon for her ideas, rather than the drawings themselves.

Realism

Moving from representation to perception

Soldier and tank by Kamil, age 8 years, 1 month

As early as age five but more often around seven or eight years of age, your child will become concerned with making his pictures look "right" in relation to how he believes things look in the real world. Figure 49 shows how children ages six to eight have worked hard to combine realistic shapes to make pictures of planes and boats. This need arises mainly through your child's desire to communicate with others through his drawings. No longer content with satisfying only himself, he has also begun the business of making his ideas clear and acceptable to others. His plea to "help me make it look real" is quite serious: he has identified a problem in his way.

Unfortunately, most parents have no idea how to help their child. "It looks okay to me" certainly does not solve the quandary posed by a drawing such as the one in figure 50. What can you do?

First and most important, you must reinspire your child's confidence in the abstract design skills he has naturally developed, even when his subjects are realistic. Help him understand that any realistic subject is still a set of shapes and patterns, and *so is a drawing*. In many cases, if you can find a reference of the subject, such as a photograph, or if you can take a closer look at the subject in nature, you can help him see the real shapes and designs that make up the subject and help him match them to the shapes in his drawing.

In situations like figure 50, your child may need to think more about how the appearance of an object changes depending on his point of view. He may actually be trying to include more than one viewpoint in his drawing, which will lead to problems. You can ask him if he is looking at the subject from its side, from above, or straight on, and help him sort out the different views.

In every situation, your child will have to call on his design skills to help him fit the pieces of his drawing together in an agreeable arrangement on the paper.

Adult artists who draw or paint realistically have an extreme curiosity about the appearance of the world. They have an almost "raw" sensitivity to light and shadow, wetness and dryness, smoothness and roughness, depth and projection, and so on. In order to shift to this *perceptual* state of drawing, your child's ability to manage the larger issues of composition or design at the same time must be well developed.

However, I also believe that children are expected (and themselves expect) to draw realistically long before they are developmentally capable of certain kinds of abstract thinking such as vanishing-point perspective, overlapping, and the way that objects

Figure 49. In these four drawings, children ages six to eight grapple
with the shapes that make up realistic subjects.

appear to grow smaller in the distance. For this reason, with children ages 7 to 10 I
stress the following "drawing ingredients" in order of importance: the arrangement or
balance of different subjects and shapes on the page (realistic or not); the connection
of these subjects so that they look like they belong in the same drawing; the story-
telling or action element of the picture; and the realistic rendering of proportions,
texture, and perspective *last*.

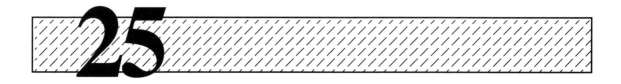

Understanding Manuel's drawing

What a wonderful *design* figure 50 is! Everything in this picture is balanced. The two sideways buildings on the far right are balanced by the sideways house centered opposite them. The central roadway, divided down the middle by a dotted line and bordered by two vertical rows of sidewalks, is surrounded by a wavy border of lawn or hedges. The four mountain peaks at the top frame the scene and hold the picture together. If you turn the drawing so that it is on its side, you can see how symmetrically each of the buildings is designed as well.

I am particularly impressed by the intuitive placement of the bumpy markings on the road, the four bird symbols, and the dots on the mountains and in the sky. Each of these marks is purposeful, and the drawing becomes unbalanced if you cover any one of them with your thumb.

Talking with Manuel about his drawing

When I spoke with Manuel, however, he was very unhappy with his perspective and sensed that something was "wrong." I reassured him that a picture like this one is not wrong because it is a design that is very well balanced, and I pointed out the various ways and places he had done so. Because Manuel kept insisting that he meant it to be "real" and not just an abstract design, I asked him if he would like to learn about point of view.

Point of view is one of the first decisions that an artist makes when he begins a picture. Before he starts to draw, the artist imagines the view he is going to show. I explained to Manuel that his picture couldn't be "corrected" after it was drawn because it didn't begin with a point of view; it began with a set of marks that were added onto until it was finished.

I would not ask a child of seven, eight, or nine years to tackle a realistic drawing with large-scale perspective, such as receding roadways and buildings, before he had some simple instruction with point-of-view exercises. Learning perspective techniques is meaningless unless the child understands that "perspective" is a result of

Figure 50. A street design by Manuel, age 7 years, 9 months

one *particular view* out of dozens of possible views. And that kind of knowledge is very abstract and advanced for many children under age 10.

Suggestions for learning about perspective

You can help your child get a preliminary grip on the idea of perspective with some simple point-of-view exercises. He could start with the following suggestions:

■ Draw a shoe from a side view, then draw it again from a top view, then draw a bottom view of the sole.

■ Draw a doll from the front and again from the back. What kinds of things show in each view?

■ Draw a car from a side view. Then cut three pictures of cars out of a magazine and discuss these questions: Do the magazine pictures show side views of the cars? Or do they show part of the side views and part of the front views? Do any of them show a back view? Does the *top* of any car show? Talk about what part of each car is closest. For example, if someone walked straight into the photo, which part of the car would be reached first? Your child might now like to try drawing another view of a car besides a side view. Think of other good subjects to discuss with your child. You might want to look through magazines for pictures of furniture, people, and buildings. For example, try to help your child understand where the photographer was standing when he took the photo. The photographer's viewpoint is the same viewpoint that you or your child have when you look at the photo.

■ Play "pretend" games. For example, pretend you're a rocket landing or an ant crawling through the garden. What would you see? What might be below you or in front of you? In figure 51, Kamil envisioned the pilot's point of view of the runway as he landed his plane.

Figure 51. An aerial view of a rocket landing on a runway by Kamil, age 8 years, 1 month

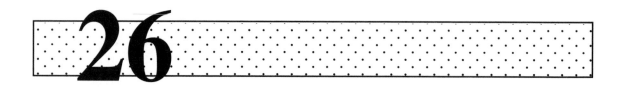

Understanding Sahhuind's drawing

In figure 52, eight-year-old Sahhuind has drawn a picture that is both a balanced design and an implied narrative or story of sorts. The picture shows a school of four fish swimming under water toward a net, with the sun and a cluster of clouds drawn above the water. You can see how the seven different subjects (the cloud cluster, the net, the four fish, and the sun) are balanced by the two open spaces in the water, one below the sun and above the fish on the far right, and the other on the bottom left leaving a space for the fish to swim "into." An elementary kind of story is set up here: Will the net catch the four fish swimming happily below it?

What struck me about this picture was Sahhuind's use of wavy overlapping lines drawn horizontally across the fish, creating a nice "underwatery" feeling of transparency.

Talking with Sahhuind about his drawing

"This picture is very realistic," I told Sahhuind. "I feel as if I'm looking through the water at the fish because of the way you drew this pattern of wavy lines across them. And you've done a good job with the clouds. Clouds often appear in lots of overlapping layers like these."

"The fish aren't very good," he said. "I don't know how to draw fish."

"Oh. I didn't really notice that," I told him, since I hadn't. His design and the attractive line patterns worked so well that the "realism" of the fish seemed unimportant. "Do you want to change the fish?" I asked. "We could go to the library and look at some pictures for ideas." In this case, only a few simple changes in body structure and parts would be needed. The drawing is otherwise well composed and integrated.

Suggestions for parents of children drawing realistically

Drawing realistic subjects such as fish depends to a large extent on your child's ability to see the subjects' outside edges clearly by either studying reference pictures

Figure 52. Fish swimming under a net by Sahhuind, age 8 years, 7 months

or observing the subjects in real life. Help your child analyze the *edges* of things and the ways their interiors are broken up into shapes. He needs to have a clear mental image of each part as well as the whole picture before he can draw accurately.

Children whose drawings are well organized may be interested in trying some wet-shading techniques, which would be helpful for showing "wateriness" in a drawing like the one in figure 52. Halfway between painting and drawing, the following techniques can be used in pictures that involve fantasy or realism:

■ Wet a piece of smooth drawing paper (*not* construction paper) and then have your child draw on it with a water-soluble or washable felt pen. Ask him to do an experimental drawing first just to see what happens, then plan ahead before starting the next drawing.

■ On dry paper, have him use a water-soluble felt pen – or one labeled "washable" – to make another drawing. Then use a paintbrush and water to shade the edges.

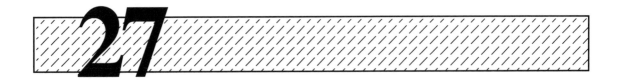

Understanding Lindsey's drawing

Lindsey has "hidden" at least six sea creatures in her bubble design (figure 53). What a labor of love this drawing must have been to complete, and what a rhythmic optical effect is set up by the tightly knit areas of different-sized bubbles. Look at one area at a time and see how the groups of bubbles change size. This drawing is a good example of an interlocking design that, while obviously more sophisticated, is very similar in mentality to Vanessa's and Jane's drawings in figure 19 and 20.

At the age of eight, Lindsey is still able to make her picture work as a design and to provide realistic accuracy where it counts. The shells of the three turtles, drawn from memory, show that she has observed and remembered their patterns and markings. The two crabs have the expected claws and legs.

Talking with Lindsey about her drawing

As your child becomes more interested in realistic detail or "scientific" accuracy, help her maintain her knack for design as an integrated part of her drawing. If she loses sight of her design, the subjects, no matter how realistically or accurately drawn, will become mere academic studies. The element of composition or *presentation* is so important for the drawing's visual impact.

You can encourage her by commenting on the design as well as the subjects. In Lindsey's case I might say, "You've camouflaged all the animals by putting bubbles around them. That was a good idea. Look at how the bubbles just fit around them."

Suggestions for being inventive with realism

■ Encourage your child to develop backgrounds and contexts for her realistic subjects. She may begin a drawing with a realistically drawn eagle, for example, then need help brainstorming ideas for its surroundings. Ask her to picture the scene it is in. Does she imagine the eagle against the sky, in a forest, or in front of some close-up rocks? Can she design a background from her imagination, or does she want to

Figure 53. An underwater design with realistic turtles by Lindsey, age 8 years, 6 months

look at some reference material to guide her? Is the eagle real, or does it come from an imaginary land? If it is imaginary, who or what else might be in that fantasy land?

■ Alternatively, encourage your child to develop ideas for "all-over" patterns like the one in figure 53 and then add subject matter to them. For example, what else could be encased in a pattern of bubbles? What could be seen through the bare branches of a tree?

If your child is imaginative and inventive like Lindsey, encourage her to try the following drawing techniques:

■ Use only dots made with a felt pen to draw a sea urchin or a rock. No cheating – there are no lines allowed, just dots. The dots can be big or small (two different felt pens can be used) and spaced in different ways – close together or farther apart. Where the dots are spaced close together, the areas will look darker. Darker areas can be used to show shadows, depth, or places where the surface indents.

■ Do a realistic drawing using one continuous line. She can draw something imaginary for the first one, then choose a simple subject that is stationary – such as a shoe, a flower, or a work tool – for a second drawing. Have her place the pen anywhere on the paper and try to keep going, without lifting the pen, until all the edges are drawn both inside and out. She will need to look closely at the edges and change direction when they do. Just for fun, have her draw a portrait of a person this way. The person who is serving as the subject may not be able to sit still for very long, so your child will have to catch the "ins" and "outs" of the profile and clothing quickly, as John did in figure 54.

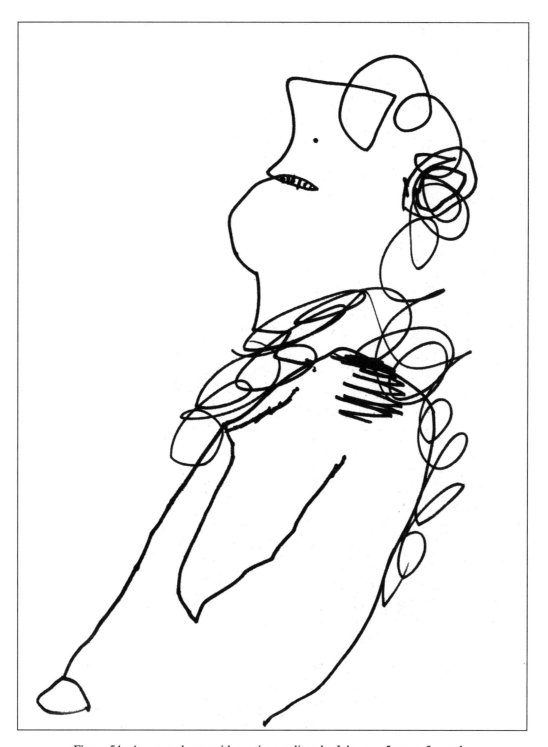

Figure 54. A person drawn with continuous lines by John, age 5 years, 3 months

Understanding Darlene's drawing

Older children now have the drawing skills to capture on paper the images that attract them. Figure 55 is a very typical portrait by 12-year-old Darlene. You can see that she has gone to a great deal of trouble to convey details where she feels they count. The girl's hair is carefully shaped and parted, her earrings clearly show clusters of beads, and great care has been taken in the placement of the flower pattern on the girl's jacket. The fingers and nails of the visible hand are carefully drawn.

There are minor awkward places in this drawing – the spacing of the facial features and the length of the arms, hands, and torso in relation to the size of the head – but overall, Darlene's ability to convey a realistic portrait is quite good. The markings on the face which show the edges of the nose, as well as the lines alongside the mouth, are clues that Darlene drew this picture from life rather than from her imagination, or that she copied it from a photo. These are both valid ways of doing a portrait.

Talking with Darlene about her drawing

I was interested to know why Darlene drew this portrait. Since the drawing wasn't obviously a self-portrait, I asked her, "Do you know this person?" She showed me a picture of a model from a magazine ad and said that she drew her because she was pretty. She didn't find anything in the background she wanted to include, so I asked her if she could imagine a background she would like.

Copying an attractive image, whether it is a person, a car, or a duck, is often a good starting point for older children, since their natural desire to copy is strong. But it is very important that children be encouraged to find a way to take the image and make it their own, perhaps by placing it in a different scene or situation or by drawing variations of it.

Figure 55. A portrait copied by Darlene, age 12 years, 4 months

Suggestions for making drawings personal

■ A child at this stage needs a sketchbook for documenting the things that attract her. She may fill the book with drawings like Elizabeth's in figure 56 or Stephens's in figure 57. The constant repetition of certain kinds of images may lead parents to exclaim, "Can't you draw anything *else*?" However, these children are working hard at mastering the ideas of *alike* and *different* in their series of images. At this stage of their artistic development, the content of their drawings is not as important as the fact that they have a strong desire to explore similarities and differences between shapes, proportions, and details.

As your child explores variations of single images, it is important to encourage her to occasionally place her images in a scene. Here are some ideas that may help her experiment with contexts as well as make her drawings personal.

■ Draw a portrait of a person surrounded by some of his or her favorite things. Your child can plan ahead by imagining whether the person is standing or seated; whether she is seen from the side, front, or back; whether he is in front of, beside, or behind some of his favorite things.

■ Draw a *fantasy* portrait of a friend or family member. Help your child start by thinking about the things that best represent that person, such as personal possessions; things the person dreams about doing or having; places the person has been; or clothes the person might like to wear. Then help her imagine how everything will be placed or spaced in her drawing. She can think of this picture as a design involving large and small objects. As she works and revises her design, she can lay a fresh sheet of paper over the last sheet and trace the parts of the drawing she wants to keep.

■ Your child can draw herself in the room of her dreams. She can first imagine what this room would look like – a video or computer room, a fantastic bedroom, or a poolside party lounge, for example. What is she doing in this room? Is anyone else there? It is easiest to plan the large things first, such as the corners of the walls and the edges of the floor; openings, doorways or steps; and furniture, rugs, and recreation equipment. She will need to think about the *proportions* or relative sizes of one thing to another, and finish with the details.

Figure 56. Exploring the concepts of "alike" and "different" through hair-styling ideas. Elizabeth, age 12 years, 4 months

Figure 57. A page from the sketchbook of Steven, age 11 years, 11 months

Questions & Answers

When I try to show my daughter, who is eight, how to draw something, it never looks right to her. What should I do?

Be sure to talk with her first, because she may have a different image in mind than you do. For example, discuss the point of view she wants to take, what will be in front and what will be behind, how big the different parts will be on the page, and what they will look like. Try to develop a clear mental picture of the subject together.

■

Our nine-year-old son only wants to draw war planes and war vehicles. How can we get him to draw other things?

When your son becomes attracted to other things, he will draw them. For now, talk to him about his war drawings. You may find they are more varied than you think! You can also encourage him to put action and movement into his drawings.

■

My daughter wants everything she draws to look "real." Should I make her try to use her imagination more?

If your daughter is learning that it is possible to draw things so that they look real, there is probably no stopping her. Encourage her to draw from ideas, feelings, and subjects in her own life so that her realistic drawings will be personal.

■

We think our daughter is really talented. Should she go to art school?

If she wants to go to art school, send her – whether you think she's talented or not. Try to choose the kind of class and environment that would appeal to your child and her personality.

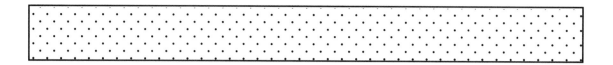

Our son is 10 and spends all of his time alone in his room drawing. Do you think this is good for him?

Your child may be on a drawing "binge" in the same way other children may obsessively shoot baskets or play Nintendo for an extended period of time. Many children get hooked on drawing in their middle years.

■

My child has trouble remembering how things look when he tries to draw them. Do you have any tips for improving visual memory? He is 11 years old.

To help your child remember shapes and parts of objects, teach him to think about how the objects feel, move, and work. To help him remember proportions, teach him to think in terms of relative sizes: How much bigger is one thing than another?

Before shading a drawing, it will help if he marks his paper to indicate where the light is coming from; the shading will all be on the other side. Surface details such as colors, textures, and patterns are harder to remember. Teach your child to use references in books or nature as a professional artist would. You can learn more about these different elements in my book *Teach Your Child to Draw*.

■

Every time our eight-year-old draws, she barely begins, then stops and says it's no good. How can we help her?

Be specific. If there is anything at all you understand in her drawings, point it out and tell her why. This will let her know she's communicating with you in spite of her fears. You can also talk about *different* ways she could finish the drawings, so that she understands there is no "right" way.

Cartoons

Combining fantasy and realism

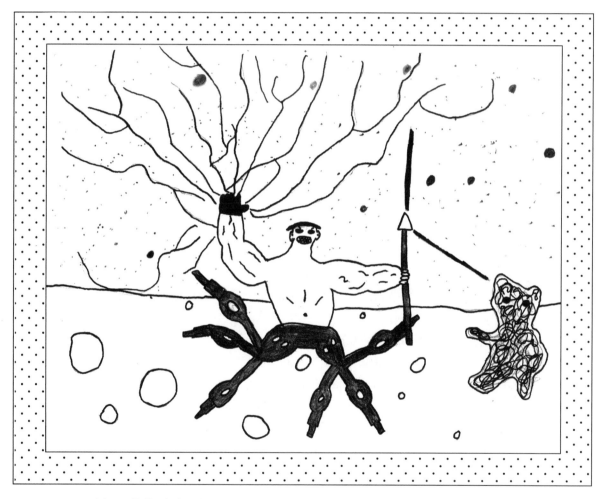

A beautifully designed and patterned original cartoon by Mark, age 12 years, 2 months

At any age in your child's life, there may come a time when he or she is only interested in drawing cartoons. Cartoons may be copied from popular commercial characters, or they may be original. In both cases, your child can learn a great deal when he draws cartoons. I don't believe that this art form in itself is bad, since cartoons combine aspects of design, fantasy, and realism.

When a commercial cartoon image such as a Teenage Mutant Ninja Turtle is new on the market, it is very attractive to children. They try to "own" it by copying it exactly as it was originally designed. It is interesting to notice how an image often works its way down through the social age groups until the four- and five-year-olds are the last to "acquire" it.

Unlike the early symbols of hearts, flowers, and rainbows that your child copied from his friends, cartoons can be hard to imitate. Your child not only has to think about proportions but also look for symmetry between parts. In drawing the Ninja Turtles in figure 58, for example, each child struggled to show the relative sizes of the arms and legs in proportion to the heads and torsos.

Children will also try to identify a set of symbolic marks for drawing the image. In each picture in figure 58, a simple cross has been drawn on the chest to show the shell division, and two straight lines have been drawn across the head and extended to create a flying scarf. Each child worked out a simplified *system* for understanding the image, and this is an important developmental step toward learning to abstract other images in the real world.

Your child will probably not stop drawing a popular cartoon character until he sees that it is no longer popular or until he has mastered a system to his satisfaction. You can encourage your child to be creative by placing popular cartoons in a context or against an original background. He can also work the image into a design of other shapes.

Drawing original cartoons is not as common, but most children receive little encouragement to create their own. This is unfortunate, as most children are capable of incredibly elaborate, detailed, and dramatic ideas of their own. Drawing cartoons can give your child a chance to place the likely next to the unlikely, to use the real in the service of the unreal, and to explore different fantasies and situations. Most importantly, drawing cartoons can help your child develop innovative solutions for showing action.

Figure 58. Four versions of a popular cartoon character, each drawn by a six- or seven-year-old boy.

Understanding Thomas's drawing

Figure 59 is a wonderful design of lines by six-year-old Thomas. Like Megan in figure 37, Thomas has broken his drawing space into flat, graphic areas. He has used a combination of horizontal lines that are wavy and diagonal lines that zigzag. The diagonal lines give the picture a strong sense of movement because they move on an angle *across* the grain of the paper. Understanding the cartoon figures may even be unnecessary to the drawing's overall visual appeal.

Almost centered in the bottom half of the picture is the "bad guy" with long arms and legs extending down from his head. He is the focal point for most of the lines in this drawing. As Thomas said, "Everybody's shooting things at him." The "good guys" – the small head-shaped figure to the left and the egg-shaped figure above – are "dropping wet stuff down so the bad guy slips."

Talking with Thomas about his drawing

Talking with most six-year-olds about their drawing is incredibly easy because they don't *stop* talking, even while they're drawing. Thomas's conversation was non-stop "zapping this" and "going to really *pow* him that," as he practically acted out animated cartoon sequences before my eyes. Try to understand your young child's cartoons in the context of a process of *acting out* ideas.

Suggestion for parents of young children who draw cartoons

■ School-age children are very interested in themes of predicament, danger, threat, escape, and revenge, all of which make superb subject matter for cartoons. You can capitalize on your young child's energy and understanding of story sequences by helping him develop his own set of characters that represent the "good," the "bad," and the "savior." Simple shapes like Thomas's are good because they allowed him to focus on the action and special effects. One enterprising teacher had her class draw their own versions of the "Mister" characters.

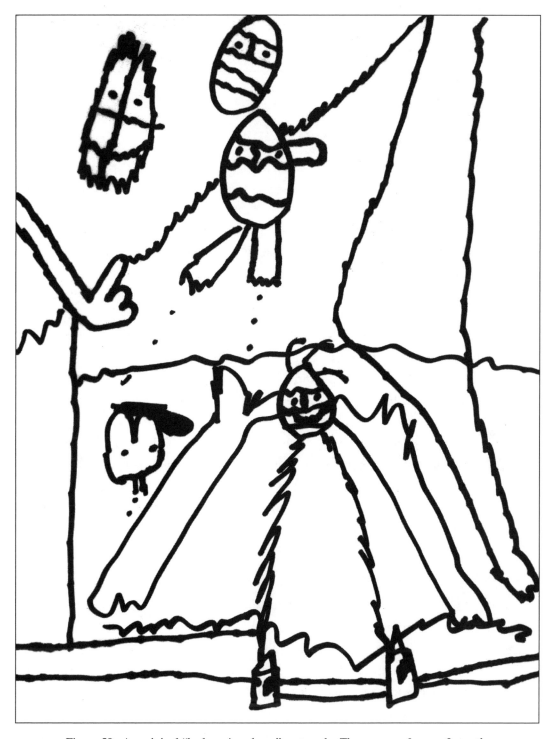

Figure 59. An original "bad guy/good guy" cartoon by Thomas, age 6 years, 9 months

Understanding Adam's drawing

Many parents are quite upset when their children draw only cartoons, and they find it hard to understand why these images are so important to children. The problem may truly lie in the generation gap between what parents and children see as "real," since realism to young children isn't just about things from everyday life. It may not even include such adult drawing subjects as bouquets of flowers and bowls of fruit.

For example, although the subject matter of a drawing like the one in figure 60 is taken from currently popular cartoon imagery and not from real life, to children such things are "real" because there is a right way and a wrong way to draw them. Their friends know this, even if adults don't! Figure 60 shows one of the Teenage Mutant Ninja Turtles standing in front of three of the four tunnels that lead to the sewers where they live. The brick ground of the sewer is under the turtle's feet, and curved over his head is a dripping sewer pipe. The chest of the figure was originally divided into sections, but Adam filled it in solidly when the pattern didn't come out "right."

Six-year-old Adam has, nonetheless, made a recognizable drawing of a known cartoon image, which is remarkable for a boy his age. He created a design of various well-balanced elements like the tunnels and the Ninja Turtle and at the same time he applied realistic thinking by evaluating their proportions.

Talking with Adam about his drawing

If your child draws something that is unfamiliar to you, it will be hard for you to encourage him or offer suggestions unless you understand the drawing first. Adam drew this picture with great confidence and steady concentration, but he was very apologetic when he gave it to me. "Yeah, I sort of like it," he admitted, "but the arms aren't right. They're too long, and there should be four tunnels, not three. I ran out of room for the other one."

It was important for Adam to explain this drawing and its problems to me so that I could learn more about his subjects and what he had intended. On the other hand, it

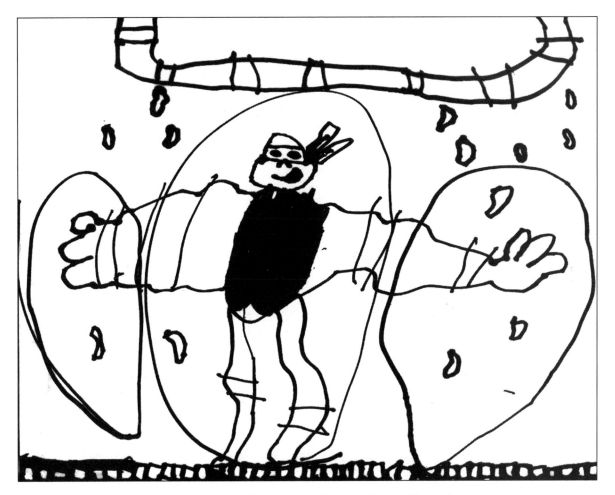

Figure 60. A Ninja Turtle by Adam, age 6 years, 10 months

was important for me to encourage him by pointing out how well he balanced the three tunnels, the pipe above, and the border of bricks below, and how well the drips were placed to hold all the parts together. "This is a really good composition," I told him. "You've thought about all the parts. If the arms and the tunnels really bother you, you could do what an artist does: put a clean sheet of paper over the top of this drawing and correct those things. Or would you rather try a different drawing?" Like Adam, your child needs to know that nothing in art ever has to be final.

It is interesting to compare six-year-old Adam's drawing in figure 60 to eleven-year-old Steven's drawing in figure 61. There is a great sense of freedom and a delight of design in Adam's drawing. However, because Steven is much older, his figures are more realistic in that they have better proportions and are more informative about costumes and anatomy. It certainly doesn't matter whether his figures happen to be wearing what adults might consider "weird" outfits. Steven has obviously worked hard at conveying information about realism through such details as muscles and the folds of clothing, and this is important knowledge he can apply to drawing figures from real life.

Although the styles and technical aptitude of the two boys are obviously quite different, in both cases I would say to them, "You drew these things as if they were real. Could you show me how they would look if they were *doing* something real? What might that be?" The following suggestions may be helpful to your child in making his cartoons more realistic.

Suggestions for getting the most out of cartoons

■ Encourage your child to draw figures from different viewpoints, including unusual ones. For example, he can draw from above looking down on the subjects, from behind as they crawl away, or from the side as they twist and fall upside-down. The sheer delight that adult artists have in drawing the extreme contortions of figures in action is what gave birth to superhero comics in the first place. Help your child see that there are many alternatives besides side views and front views.

■ Encourage your child to place his figures in a context. Do this by helping him visualize an environment *first*, the action or narrative second, and the figures last. He can visualize the background or foreground (since these surroundings may be in front of the figure and partially block or "hide" it) by thinking in terms of geographic extremes such as chasms, fantastic dunes and peaks, or sharp and broken edges. Also, encourage him to think in terms of extreme action. For example, what would an apparently hopeless situation be? What or who could save it?

■ Watch animated cartoon programs with your child and study the changing effects of distance and point of view on the characters. Discuss your observations and have him work them into his drawings.

■ Be sure your child has materials that are suitable for more detailed or advanced drawing. Children try to match the size of the drawing medium to the paper, so if the paper they normally use is 8^1/$_2$" x 11" they may prefer to draw with a fine-tip felt pen or a sharp pencil. Wide felt pens may be very difficult to use on such a small scale.

Figure 61. Superheroes by Steven, 11 years, 10 months

■ Drawing an object also helps your child develop a mental image of it. If he is learning to perceive such fine details as the teeth on the chainsaw or the folds in the pants on the right-hand figure in figure 61, he will find that drawing with a fine-tip felt pen or a sharp pencil results in a more accurate *mental* representation and thus a more accurate drawing.

■ Visit an art supply store to buy either sheets of illustration board which have a hard, smooth, hot-press finish, or technical board. Your child can cut standard 20" x 30" or 30" x 40" sheets down to smaller, more table-manageable sizes. The surfaces of these types of boards are ideal for making detailed drawings such as the one in figure 61.

■ Help your child select a good technical pen or Rapidograph for drawings that have fine detail.

Understanding Tom's drawing

Figure 62 is based on a commonplace scene in everyday life, which is subject matter that children do not often choose voluntarily. In this case, the cartoon shows a man waiting at a bus stop. It includes very perceptive details, such as the gutter in the street and the grooves in the sidewalk. The bench, the curb, and the top of the bus stop sign are all drawn in perspective, showing a viewpoint from slightly above.

What is unusual about this drawing is the fanciful turn of imagination which led Tom to add eyes peering through the windows, gun barrels protruding from the doorway and vents, and bullets coming out of the guns toward the unsuspecting man. Like Cheehan in figure 39, 12-year-old Tom has a dry sense of humor that enables him to claim any scene as his own.

Talking with Tom about his drawing

Did Tom draw this scene entirely from his imagination, or did he base it on a photograph? I was impressed to discover that he had "made it up." He had imagined the perspective of many objects in the scene, such as the change of direction in the sidewalk grooves at the curb. I pointed out how the hidden gunmen change the otherwise quiet tone of the drawing and liven up the extremely calm and perfectly balanced composition. They are a "surprise" element in this cartoon.

Suggestions for drawing cartoons about real life

■ Encourage your child to draw scenes that are set in surroundings from his daily life. By the age of 10, he is entering a period of intense social awareness and can explore different sociological themes, such as inner-city violence; suburban life in neighborhoods and malls; or rural isolation. What kinds of action pictures could be set in his environment? Are there any real or observed dangers in his neighborhood? Encourage him to draw them in cartoons, as cartoons can help your child express his feelings about things that alarm or threaten him.

Figure 62. A realistic cartoon by Tom, age 12 years

Understanding Aaron's drawing

Figure 63 is the playing board for an original game by 11-year-old Aaron, and I have no idea what it means. However, as a drawing I really like it.

The picture is a mystery, full of dozens of details to think about. There are many small, clear, and charming creatures spaced throughout the maze of interlocking background shapes. Tiny staircases, tunnels, and a rope ladder lead the eye from space to space, with many obstacles to consider along the way, such as missing ladder rungs, a morning star on one of the staircases, and speeding knives. Small threats in the forms of a skull, a bomb, and giant lobster claws are mixed together with small treats: bags of money, a treasure chest, and a door that leads to "Fun." A convoluted kind of story is obviously at work here, with cause-and-effect linkages and entrapments. Wouldn't you like to play this game?

Suggestions for professional-looking drawing projects

■ Help your child take his artwork to its furthest conclusion. If he draws pages for a book, why not have them laminated, coil-bound, or put in a cover? If you have access to a computer, you can create text for the book. Use a desktop publishing program to create different typestyles. Have the text laser-printed if possible, then assemble the text and glue it in place on the drawings.

■ Photocopiers can be used to enlarge black-and-white drawings to 11" x 17" to create posters or game boards. The images could then be colored in with felt pens. Aaron, for example, could glue the enlarged version of his drawing onto a cardboard backing and do the same for the accompanying game cards he also drew. The whole set could then be laminated. This would make it possible for him to play his board game with his friends.

■ Have your child color his original drawing, then have it reproduced on a color laser copier. Multiple copies could be reproduced, cut out, and mounted on cards to make holiday greetings or party invitations. Large original drawings up to 11" x 17" can easily be reduced to a card size on a color copier for an unusual and personal gift.

Figure 63. An original game board by Aaron, age 11 years, 11 months

Questions & Answers

My 12-year-old is very talented at cartooning, and all of his friends envy him. But he says he "hates" doing art at school.

The artwork that your child is asked to do in his classroom may not match his interest in drawing right now. Cartooning is just one form of art, but to children at a certain stage it can seem like the only way to draw. Certainly cartooning provides a lot of freedom for expressing action, emotions, and feelings of control. In time your child will learn that other forms of art, including those done at school, can do the same.

■

Our 10-year-old daughter only wants to draw "fashion" outfits for girls. How can we encourage her to try other subjects?

Help her finish this phase of her interest first. Buy a binder or small portfolio with plastic sleeves to display and save her drawings. Perhaps she would like to make photocopies of her fashion figures and cut them out for younger children to play with. She could also sponsor a "fashion show" and invite her friends over to draw with her. Why not have a pretend runway show?

■

My son does very complicated lettering in the margins of his books but doesn't draw real things.

Lettering is also a form of drawing and painting. Very ornate examples can be found in such different sources as old illustrated manuscripts, computer-graphic designs, and subway graffiti. There are many books in the library which will help you understand how lettering carries visual messages or feelings. This sounds like a good design outlet for your son.

■

Our 10-year-old son is a perfectionist about his drawings. He draws things over and over until he gets them right. Is this natural?

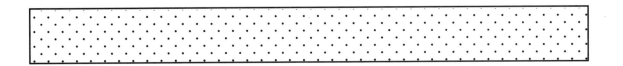

Many professional adult artists do dozens of small sketches or studies before they are satisfied. Others work in series that explore similar aspects of the same idea. Your son is learning to refine his thoughts and ideas at this stage. You can show interest by discussing his changes with him.

■

I teach art to grades six and seven. Most of the students draw pretty well, but they have a lot of trouble when they paint. Do you have any suggestions?

Drawing and painting techniques have one thing in common: both are used to make marks on a surface. First, teach your students to *draw* by using shorter and more varied kinds of marks to fill in different areas, rather than always outlining areas with single lines such as those used to draw cartoons. It will then be easier for them to understand how paintings are made up of many varied strokes of paint.

Find reproductions of paintings that show the brushstrokes clearly. Examine them with your students and point out the different lengths and directions of the strokes. Remind them that paintings (just like drawings) don't happen by magic – someone has to put the paint on!

■

My children have never shown much interest in art. I guess they don't have any talent, like me. Is it too late to teach them something?

Expose them to art in the world around them. There is almost nothing man-made that an artist hasn't had a hand in designing or illustrating: from landscape design to interior decoration, from the textures and patterns of clothes and furnishings to the designs of our homes, schools, and cars, as well as the choice of type, photographs, and illustrations in books, magazines, or anything else that is printed. Perhaps your children will become interested in trying new areas of art – and so may you!

Action

A busy action scene with lots of cause-and-effect relationships by Tom, age 11 years, 3 months

Possibly the most endearing children's drawings are those that portray action or movement. Whether a four-year-old is activating her whole arm or even her whole body to transfer energy to her drawing paper, or whether an eight-year-old is inventing solutions for showing different stages of movement in more representational images, children of all ages attempt to convey movement in their artwork.

Most adults accept that a drawing is static, which means that it can't really move. Many adult artists try to show the effect of action in their pictures by "freezing" or catching it at one point of movement, much like a photographer does. Other artists are able to arrange colors and composition in ways that create a sense of movement in the eyes of the viewer.

Children are much more direct. Young children may use arrows, dotted lines, or other directional marks to make their schemes perfectly clear. Scribbles can be used to depict whirls of movement or even the *results* of movement that can't be expressed in shapes. In figure 64, for example, seven-year-old Jayme used scribbles to show skate marks all over the ice where there had been movement earlier in the hockey game. Even though the two figures don't move, these marks (together with the image of the goalie's broken stick) give the whole picture a feeling of motion. Children also find drawing particularly useful for showing things that can't be seen but which obviously exist, like the musical notes coming out of the princess's throat in figure 66.

These young artists are also fearless. Intuitively and instinctively responding to the challenges of drawing objects that are traveling, falling, or exploding, children often come up with ingenious solutions. They may repeat a figure in stages of movement (see figure 65), use diagonal lines or arrangements effectively to make their drawings dynamic (see figure 67), or experiment with such cartoonlike conventions as drawing lines in the air around objects to indicate movement.

Older children can take the potential of a drawing to its limit. For example, instead of merely drawing rain lines at the top of a picture or simply giving all the people umbrellas, they are able to show flooding, reflections on wet surfaces, or shininess. Their drawings eventually become more refined as they learn to replace exaggerated facial expressions with flailing limbs, to use vanishing-point perspective to indicate the way objects become smaller as they travel into the distance, or to use new materials and techniques for shading and blurring in order to show movement.

Figure 64. Scribbled skate marks on the ice give this hockey game, won by Wayne Gretzky (99) and the Los Angeles Kings, a feeling of movement. Jayme, age 7 years, 2 months

It is always exciting to see the advanced development in children at this stage, but it is also sad to see their fascinating and instinctive solutions begin to disappear. Be sure to save your child's precious early drawings of movement as a reminder of their charm and inventiveness.

Understanding Andre's drawing

On the left in figure 65 is a castle tower with a girl – possibly a princess – standing on top. A "bad guy" has knocked her off the tower, and the five figures drawn down the right side of the tower show the girl in various stages of falling through the air. The "bad guy" himself has also met with fate and is seen upside down on the far right, falling through the air. In the sky above, a battle of the elements is being waged.

While the content of this drawing is Andre's fantasy, the forms used to *express* the content are a mixture of the representational and the innovative. For example, the expression on the princess's face changes as she falls, but the lines drawn to represent her hair remain consistent with the force of gravity. When she is upright, her hair hangs down; when she is upside down, her hair still hangs down. These representational observations are nicely combined with expressive scribbles and "zapping" marks to show the movement of light and energy in the air.

Talking with Andre about his drawing

Drawings full of life and information such as Andre's are good candidates for discussion. From the expressive marks to the perilous situation, there were many things to comment on. Like Daniel's drawing in figure 25, be sure to offer some specific comments on the contents of your child's art, even if you're not sure you're right.

Suggestion for parents of children drawing movement

■ Shop at an art store for supplies that are useful when drawing action, such as watercolor pencil crayons for drawings that can be shaded with water and a brush; brightly colored pastels that can be smudged for effect; or graphite pencils that can also be shaded with water. Marks made by all felt pens labeled "washable" or "water soluble" can also be blended with water and a brush.

Figure 65. A princess falling from her castle by Andre, age 9 years, 5 months

Understanding Alison's drawing

Figure 66 was originally done in color with brightly colored and fluorescent felt pens. It shows a princess wearing a bejeweled crown and singing for her "true love." Her beautiful singing voice is shown in her throat with turquoise, purple, green, and magenta confettilike lines radiating from a red heart. Flying out of her voice and into the air are musical notes and treble clefs that fill and decorate the background space around her head.

Seven-year-old Alison has used several different styles to draw this picture and has unified them intuitively and beautifully. Scribbles are used to draw the hair, the cheeks, and the notes on the bottom right; carefully curled lines are arranged on the forehead for bangs and echoed in both the curving treble clefs and the curly hearts on the left side; shorter lines and dots decorate the voice and the crown. This very simple picture is extremely appealing.

Talking with Alison about her drawing

Alison was in a group of seven-year-old girls who were drawing pictures of one another – or at least "naming" pictures for each other, which is a great compliment in the middle years. Alison told me this was a picture of her friend, "Princess Mariam."

Suggestion for colored drawings

■ Buy "smelly" markers. Young children love to draw with a full range of scented colored markers, from "lemon" for yellow to "grape" for purple. I have found that while using these markers children ages six to nine tend to draw longer and try out more unusual subjects, to create designs and patterns instead of worrying about drawing realistically, and to complete their drawings in a more finished or evenly composed way. Be forewarned, however, that many brands of these markers do not wash out of clothing easily – or off the noses of preschoolers, who will probably sniff more than they draw!

Figure 66. A princess singing for her true love by Alison, age 7 years, 10 months

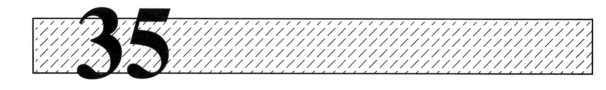

Understanding Philip's drawing

A winged dinosaur-like creature hovers in the air while planes shoot at its chest and tail and people on the ground launch firebombs at its tail and feet. Ten-year-old Philip drew this side view in figure 67 from his imagination, and was able to show the three-dimensional shapes of the dinosaur's arms and legs by planning ahead and overlapping them. The firebombs are directed with dotted lines and hit the dinosaur with scribbled explosions. The people were drawn as stick figures, which is a symbolic system learned in later childhood as a kind of shorthand and which is used when shapes or recognizable features are unimportant. In figure 67, they serve as a handy way to rapidly express the idea of the picture.

The strength of this drawing lies in the numerous types of movement lines that direct explosions toward the dinosaur. Notice how they cross the paper diagonally, or at an angle, which is the most effective way to create a feeling of movement in a picture. The resulting network of design gives this picture a strong base.

Talking with Philip about his drawing

A drawing like this one could only be done spontaneously and with great confidence and style. "Look how well you drew the action," I commented to Philip. "All the different lines and explosions make me feel I'm right there in the battle. Your proportions are good in this picture. The small people and the tiny planes make me feel the dinosaur is really huge."

Suggestion for a series of action drawings

■ Suggest that your child plan a video or an animated story. (A drawing like the one in figure 67 would make an ideal scene in an ongoing story.) Children over the age of six or seven are capable of taking a unique image or character and putting it in a variety of situations through a series of drawings, a cartoon strip, or even a set of images planned as a "storyboard" for making a film or video – real or fantastic.

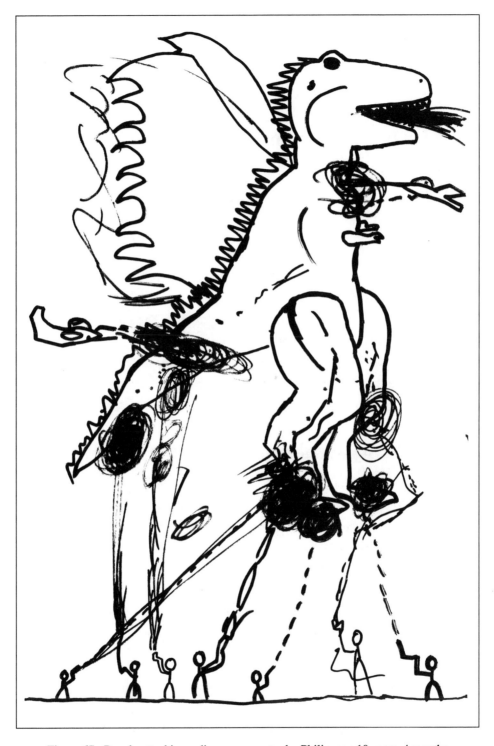

Figure 67. People attacking a dinosaur monster by Philip, age 10 years, 4 months

Understanding Steven's drawing

Eleven-year-old Steven has combined vanishing-point perspective, technological information, and a terrific imagination in this original drawing of intergalactic war.

Centered at the very top of this picture in the far distance is a jagged-metal space station. Immediately below the cockpit of the station is the circular firing station, which shoots diagonal laser beams that radiate out and divide the foreground space into sections. A closer look reveals miniature triangular destroyers around the perimeter of the station. Flying toward the space station, and therefore seen from behind, is the attacking space fleet of the "good guys." The commander of the space fleet is flying the center spacecraft with the lowered wings.

This drawing is an example of one-point perspective, in which all the lines in the drawing converge to a center point. Steven uses this device beautifully to compress a great deal of information into a small space.

Talking with Steven about his drawing

Unless you are involved with older children and adolescents in your work, you may be out of touch with themes and images your child knows well. Can you tell a space shuttle from a rocket? Can you identify four common kinds of rockets, such as a speed rocket, a cruise rocket, a rocket ship, and a destroyer? I couldn't! Steven told me about many new things through this drawing.

Suggestions for understanding your older child's images

Children today are engulfed with graphic images in a way their parents never were. Images are everywhere: on T-shirts and posters, in computer games, and on animated television shows. Three-dimensional images on television turn, change angle, recede and advance, and multiply so rapidly that they seem to exist in the fourth dimension. Try to spend more time with your older child observing and understanding the imagery that interests him.

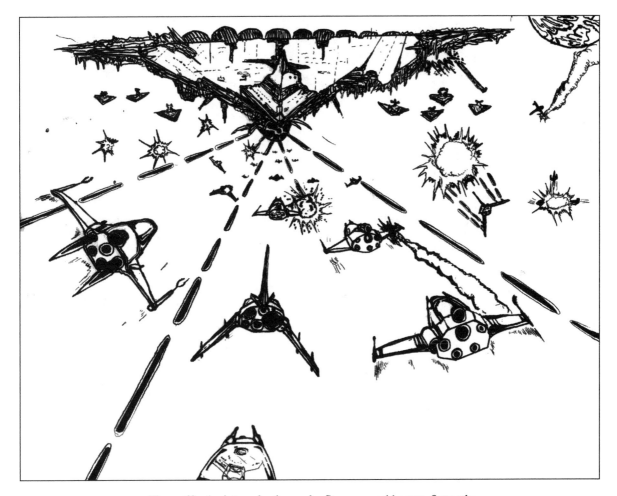

Figure 68. An intergalactic war by Steven, age 11 years, 8 months

■ Help your child examine the use of special effects and the computerized image manipulation by occasionally viewing animated programs with him. Comment on the effects you like. Some are very beautiful and others very clever.

■ Read some of his comic books and look at the different ways the artists depict motion, show changing proportions, or change their viewpoints. Study the drawing techniques as well. What kinds of marks are used for explosions? How do artists show traveling or burning? You may see these effects in your child's drawings.

■ Familiarize yourself with current fads and fashions that are important to your child. It may be difficult to truly understand and appreciate his drawings if you don't recognize the contents.

Questions & Answers

My six-year-old tells wild stories and draws furiously, but when he shows his drawings to me I don't see anything.

Trying to understand an action drawing after it is finished can be like trying to understand a rodeo by looking at the hoofprints left behind in the dust. For many young children the process is everything. Try sitting next to your son as he draws and enjoy the show!

■

Our daughter is eight and still uses a lot of scribbles in her drawings. What can I do to help her?

Children (and even many adult artists) may use scribble marks to indicate different elements such as action, weather, reflections, and textures for trees and the ground long after they are able to draw other things realistically. Encourage your child to experiment with other kinds of marks that might work in these cases. You will find more specific suggestions in my book *Teach Your Child to Draw*.

■

My son draws a lot at home and we think he is really talented. But his teacher says he never wants to draw at school, and when he does, it's not very good. Do you think he has a good teacher?

I have no idea whether he has a good teacher or not! But it is likely his reluctance has less to do with the teacher than with his need for both privacy and control over what he puts in his pictures. He may feel inhibited when he draws in front of others, or he may have trouble concentrating in the more stimulating classroom environment.

■

Our 12-year-old daughter makes all her drawings and paintings really dark, using only colors like black and red. Is this okay?

Older children are beginning to discover that colors can carry symbolic meanings. Talk to her about the meanings of the colors she uses and how colors can stand for

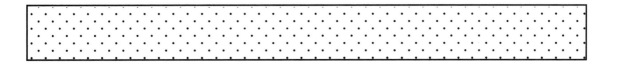

different things in different situations. For example, red can be a symbol of love on Valentine's Day and a symbol of life for the Red Cross. It can also be a danger color in animals and insects, and means "stop" when used as a traffic symbol. The color black is glamorous in an evening gown but is sad when worn at a funeral. The meanings of colors depend on the contexts.

■

My child, who is five, smears finger paints all over the table and his arms. Are there some things I can teach him to do?

Finger paints are good for making lines when children have a minimum of control. Children use them in two ways: to draw lines of paint on a clear surface, and to remove lines of paint from a smeared surface – in other words, to draw in reverse. Your son may be bored with the finger-paint stage and be ready for something like colored felt pens. These would give him maximum control over his drawings and more detail where he wants it. He will be able to express action through shapes and designs, rather than through smearing.

■

Our 10-year-old son used to draw all the time, but now he says it's "baby stuff." Is there any way we can get his interest back?

He may be interested in trying some new and more sophisticated art materials. Visit a good art supply store or an art fair to see product demonstrations. You might also want to buy some professional artists' materials, or a paint program if he likes computers. While it is important to help your child complete or master each stage of his drawing development, it is also important to sense when he is ready for some assistance to the next. Good luck!